The Palace of Morgana

and other fantasy tales

by

John Sterling

Published by Bookship, 2018.

ISBN 978-1-9996269-0-7

Introduction, cover art & design © 2018 Murray Ewing.

The Palace of Morgana
and Other Fantasy Tales

BOOKSHIP

Portrait of John Sterling, 1830. (By J. Brown.)

Wisdom's Pearl doth often dwell
Closed in Fancy's rainbow shell.
        — Sterling, "A Chronicle of England"

Contents

Introduction 9

The Palace of Morgana 15

A Chronicle of England 25

The Suit of Armour and the Skeleton 43

The Caterpillar 59

The Last of the Giants 63

The Shell 74

Zamor 78

Cydon 92

Melita: A Fragment of Greek Romance 114

The Lycian Painter 124

The Crystal Prison 134

The Sons of Iron 136

The Substitute for Apollo 142

Balthazar 148

Beatrice 155

Land and Sea 160

Introduction

One of the impulses that led Tolkien to create Middle-Earth and the whole "Legendarium" set within it was his desire to make a mythology for England, a country he felt didn't have a characteristic myth of its own. It's too much to claim that so slight a tale (certainly in comparison to *The Lord of the Rings*) as John Sterling's "A Chronicle of England" had similar ambitions, but it touches on the same territory. First published in 1840 in Blackwood's Magazine, Sterling's tale paints a poetic picture of a fairy-haunted isle, where the unending conflict between the sunlight-loving fairies and their dark, thunderous brothers, the giants, in the days before the land received its first human inhabitants seems, at times, to be a mythologising of that most English of preoccupations, the isle's ever-changing weather, and a celebration of the many delicate shades of sunlight, cloud, mist and storm that, to a Romantic-minded writer such as Sterling, lent England its own particular type of enchantment.

It's a tale that perhaps owes its greatest debt to Shakespeare, and the playfully elaborate fairy world he evokes in *A Midsummer Night's Dream*. Similarly, Sterling's 1837 tale, "The Palace of Morgana" — a virtually conflict-free idyll in which bright young things flit about the grounds of a paradisal palace, amusing themselves with displays of magic — perhaps owes something to Shakespeare's other great work of fantasy, with its magician figure possibly being a young and carefree pre-*Tempest*

Prospero.

This Shakespearean feel to what were two of the last stories Sterling wrote was a new element, both in Sterling's own writing, and the fantasy of his day, and points intriguingly at the direction he might have taken his writing, had he lived longer. Fantasy of Sterling's type, rooted in the Romantic ideal of seeking (as Shelley put it) "strange truths in undiscovered lands", and which was inspired by the darker literary fairy tales being written in Germany at the time, would be almost exclusively addressed to an audience of children throughout the rest of the nineteenth century in England (Sara Coleridge's *Phantasmion* (1837) and John Ruskin's *King of the Golden River* (1841) being two early examples), and it was not until the likes of Lord Dunsany's *King of Elfland's Daughter* (1924), and Hope Mirrlees's *Lud-in-the-Mist* (1926), that similarly enchanting fantasies were addressed to an adult audience one again. Sterling might have changed all that, but he died in 1844, aged 38, of the tuberculosis that had dogged his adult life.

Sterling was born in 1806, on the Scottish Isle of Bute, where his father, a former militia captain, rented a farm. The family moved to London in 1815, where Sterling's father became a political writer, and young John was educated at Greenwich, Blackheath and Christ's Hospital schools. During this time, as Thomas Carlyle writes in his *Life of John Sterling*:

"New brothers and sisters had been born; two little

brothers more, three little sisters he had in all; some of whom came to their eleventh year beside him, some passed away in their second or fourth: but from his ninth to his sixteenth year they all died; and in 1821 only [elder brother] Anthony and John were left."

Between 1822 and 1824, Sterling studied at the University of Glasgow, then returned to England to enter Trinity College, Cambridge. Unable to choose between a career in law, politics, the church, or letters, he left without a degree.

With a friend, the theologian and writer Frederick Denison Maurice, Sterling founded a literary magazine, The Metropolitan Quarterly. A couple of years later, the pair took on proprietorship of The Athenaeum magazine (which continued publication, in other hands, until 1921). It was here Sterling published his first fantasy tales, including the mock-Oriental "The Caterpillar" (whose main virtue is the deliberate silliness of the moral he adds at the end), the poignant fifteenth-century-set "The Last of the Giants", and "Zamor", a mix of classical history and Gothic nightmare, a kind of *Vathek*-in-miniature built from three glimpses into the life of Alexander the Great.

By this time Sterling had become a disciple of Samuel Taylor Coleridge, visiting the elder statesman of Romanticism at his home on Highgate Hill. Now in his mid-fifties and having long since ceased to produce poetry, Coleridge, in Carlyle's words, "had this dusky sublime character; and sat there as a kind of *Magus*, girt in mystery and enigma." Sterling recorded many of the conversations the two had (which, according to Carlyle — certainly no Coleridgean — would have mostly consisted of the older man rambling on various topics while Sterling listened), though these records were subsequently lost.

Sterling married Susannah Barton in 1830. A year later, the couple moved to the Caribbean island of St Vincent where, through his mother's uncle, Sterling had inherited a plantation. He hoped the climate would help with the symptoms of tuberculosis that were starting to make themselves known. But these were the days of plantations worked by slaves, and Sterling's attempts to improve the quality of life and schooling of those on his own plantation evoked ill feeling, and even persecution, from his fellow plantation-owners. A son, Edward, was born to the couple, but the family home, including Sterling's library, was destroyed in a hurricane. After fifteen months, they left St Vincent.

1833 saw the publication of Sterling's novel, *Arthur Coningsby* (which was probably written as much as five years earlier). The tale of a young man's political awakening as he experiences the turmoil of post-revolutionary France, it contained several tales embedded within its main narrative, some of a fantastic or weird nature, including the short horror story "The Crystal Prison", (whose central idea would appear in "The Hell of Mirrors" by early-20th century Japanese writer Edogawa Ranpo), and "The Sons of Iron", a short fable about metal men. These, and several other tales, were later published in their own right in the posthumous, two-volume *Essays and Tales*. (*The Palace of Morgana and Other Fantasy Tales* collects two more stories taken from *Arthur Coningsby*, "Balthazar" and "Beatrice".)

The novel was a modest success, but Sterling's growing family (a daughter, Anna, was born in March the same year) needed a more secure income, so he took up the offer of a position in the church, becoming curate at Hurstmonceux in East Sussex, where his former Cambridge tutor (and later literary executor along with Thomas Carlyle) Julius Charles Hare was vicar. (Sterling also finally completed his Bachelor of Arts degree at Cambridge before being ordained.)

He lasted just over half a year in the position. Either disagreements with the Church of England's ideas, or the dictates of his poor health, led to his resigning in February 1835. It was after this that his final series of tales, published in Blackwood's Magazine under the shared heading "Legendary Lore", began to appear, among which were his best yet, including "A Chronicle of England", "The Palace of Morgana", "The Suit of Armour and the Skeleton", and the ballad-like tale of the fateful draw of the ocean, "Land and Sea".

Double tragedy struck in 1843. Sterling received news of his mother's death and, barely two hours later, his own wife died, having recently given birth to their second daughter, Hester. He proposed to the Quaker and diarist Caroline Fox in the following year but was, by this time, in poor health, and Caroline's family advised against the match. He died in September 1844.

Care of Sterling's "literary Character and printed Writings" (as Carlyle put it) were given into the joint hands of Julius Charles Hare and Thomas Carlyle. When, in 1848, the two-volume *Essays and Tales* was published, it contained a biographical essay by Hare, and Carlyle took exception to Hare's preoccupation with "excusing and explaining" Sterling's "ecclesiastical heresies" at the expense of saying much about the man himself. In response, Carlyle wrote his own *Life of John Sterling*, which was published in 1851.

During his lifetime, Sterling's work had been championed by Ralph Waldo Emerson, who had sought an American publisher for it. Sterling's fantasy short stories draw from the same source (German Romanticism) as those of his contemporary, Edgar Allan Poe, but, though Sterling's did sometimes touch on such Gothic-Romantic topics as madness, horror, fate, and the dreadful sublime, his tales have a greater degree of light and enchantment in them, making them generally very different in tone to Poe's.

What Sterling left behind is as much about the promise of what he might have gone on to do as what he actually achieved, but his better tales — "The Last of the Giants", "The Palace of Morgana", "A Chronicle of England", "Zamor", "The Suit of Armour and the Skeleton" — certainly make them worth reading by those who like the poetic, the enchanting, and the imaginative in fantasy literature.

Sterling is a worthy addition to any fantasy reader's library.

Murray Ewing

The Palace of Morgana

(From Blackwood's Magazine, 1837)

The Palace of Morgana was vast and beautiful, with many halls and galleries of marble, jet, crystal, and lapis lazuli. Cornices of gay colours, mosaic pavements, continuous paintings of the most fanciful arabesques appeared on all sides; and through the florid windows, which in that climate needed no glass to close them, was seen the prospect of the large and lovely gardens. These were full of ancient trees, green turf, and beds of red flowers, and were divided by marble terraces from the wooded walks around. Many bright fountains played their diamond arches against the sun. All the birds of fairy-land flitted across the avenues, or rested in the foliage. Beautiful statues, and pieces of fantastic sculpture were placed here and there in those pleasant grounds, or grew like alabaster lilies from unknown seeds beneath. In sight of these fair things, many colonnades and domes rose amid the masses of foliage, for the assembling or repose of the happy inhabitants.

There, at a certain season, which grave historians have generally omitted to speak of, were a party of young men and damsels. They spent their time in singing to each other, in gathering and braiding flowers, in sports and dancing, or in enjoying their light and gay repast beneath the shade. Their life was fit for spring-time, full of courtesy and honour; and all evil was as far from the thought of those youths and ladies, as was the appearance of aught foul or unpleasing from their abode. Some of them were generally together; of these, no doubt, one clung to another more than to the rest; and there might be seen the soft sweet feelings of mutual love creeping into many hearts. Others were content to pass the hours more carelessly, conversing with all, or alternately with different persons, and taking almost as much pleasure from observing the signs of affection in those around them, as those whom they laughed at found in their own feelings. Among those whose regards and gentleness extended to all, and did not fix on any one in particular, was the young and beautiful Lady Viola. Sometimes, when a band of her friends were sitting in the dreamy noontide shadow, or wandering slowly under the twilight, she would spring among them out of a thicket with her wild and airy dance, like a wind-tossed moonbeam, scatter among them a handful of orange-flowers, and then start off again, too lightly for any foot to follow; and from some tangled depth of leaves, on the height of a rock covered with ash-boughs, her voice would be heard in free and solitary song. She was witty, and merry, and courteous; and her words and her capricious presence were pleasanter to all, than the beauty of any of her companions. But she gave equal looks to man and woman. Many hearts were entangled in the meshes of her brown hair; but on none had she ever bestowed a lock of it.

Among the noble and generous youths assembled in Morgana's palace, was one less cheerful than the rest, whom the others therefore sometimes called the Solitary; sometimes, from his powers of song, the Minstrel; and sometimes again, from the strange tales he told, and the feats he was said to have performed, the Magician. He often wandered in the woods, while the rest were sporting in the colonnades of the palace, or gathering fair nosegays in the gardens. And while they sat around a fountain, delighting themselves with song and jest and tale, he would be seen for a few moments crossing some dark avenue, and apparently lost in thought. Viola was the lady whom he chiefly sought to converse with. But her replies to him were generally light and mocking; and seldom would she remain near him, or indeed near any one, for more than an instant. Once only it was noticed that at night, when the stars were shining with peculiar beauty, and the lordly planet Jupiter seemed to rule the sky, her voice was heard in long-continued and exulting song from the summit of a wooded cliff: and, when it ceased, a pipe, known as the Magician's, answered faintly from the dark river-bed below, and, after sounding a few notes, appeared to re-awaken Viola's melody.

One afternoon the whole party were assembled under a huge horse-chestnut, covered with fan-like leaves and spring flowers. Near them was a large and finely-shaped vase of Alabaster, adorned with exquisite sculpture of Nymphs and Bacchanals. The Lady Viola was peculiarly fond of it, and took care to crown it daily with the sweetest and brightest flowers. The different parties moved towards the vase from many sides of the garden, gliding over the soft turf and the smooth marble of the terraces, with their various garments glancing brightly under the evening sun through the openings of the thick foliage. Viola came bearing in her hand some mountain heather which she had newly culled, and which she now added to the garland of the vase. The others gathered round her; and one said, while looking at the sculptured figures, "I wish I could make them move and dance."

"Such things have been done," said another.

"I wonder," exclaimed a third, "could our friend the Magician accomplish such a feat?"

"Oh!" cried several voices, "I wish he were here; I would try."

"I wish he were!" said Viola, in a low voice; and immediately the leaves of the neighbouring thicket rustled, and the Magician stood before them.

He seemed not thirty years of age. His purple dress was laced with gold; a crimson cloak hung from his shoulders; his high forehead and large black eyes were shaded by a broad cap of the same colour, from under which his long raven hair fell over his shoulders, and gave him a wizard look, at which it might almost have been fancied, from the expression of his face, that he himself was quietly smiling. He held in his hand a pipe of ivory, wrought in imitation of a reed; and from it he was accustomed to draw such sounds, as enchanted and filled with sad delight the guests of the invisible Morgana.

"You wished me here?" he said to Viola.

"Oh!" she replied, "you must have quick ears. I thought you were at the other end of the garden."

"Your wish," he said, "expressed in a fainter whisper, would have brought me from the other end of the earth."

While they spoke thus, most of those near them sat down on the grass, or on the carved and mossy-cushioned benches; and he said to Viola, — "But will you not sit, while I lie at your feet, and hear your commands?"

She was in an unusually compliant mood; for she sat down at his desire. He placed himself as he had proposed, and addressed her again: "Now, lady, how can I pleasure you?"

"Thus," she said; "we were all wishing you here, to make the figures on this Vase move, as if endowed with life."

"Is that all? I could teach a child to do that."

He placed his instrument to his lips, and began to play a tune which none of them had ever heard before. It soon grew louder; and at each return of the strain some faster and wilder movement was added to it. All eyes were fixed on the Vase, till, from the very intentness of their looks, and the strong thrilling of the music, which they felt as if it shook the earth, they hardly knew whether the marble remained immovable, or whether they themselves were not whirled around it. But after some minutes all were satisfied that the figures actually glided on; the Nymphs and Satyrs wove their arms together in the dance, and shook their thyrsuses and garlands; and while the music sank, so as to be almost inaudible, the shapes completed their circle, and were restored to their former places and attitudes.

"Wondrous!" said all present; "he is indeed a magician."

"This," he replied, "is little. It is but to have learned an old forgotten tune, which men of late years seem to have thought too good for them, and so have left it to the invisible powers."

Viola said nothing; but he ventured to look at her; and the slight softening of the eye, and the faint flush upon her cheek, overpaid him for a thousand incantations. Soon she exclaimed laughingly, "If this be so little, could you not show us some achievement of your art, which you consider really worthy of you?"

"Willingly," replied he, and drew a single peculiar note from his instrument. He then begged her to touch the ground beside him with a sprig of flowered myrtle which she held in her hand. At the sign a fountain rose from the earth, and formed a crystal dome above the Magician, dividing him from Viola. Through its dazzling colours and swift motion his form could not be distinguished. Suddenly it sank again; and he had vanished. Not a trace of him remained; and the water had left no token behind, but a few drops of dew upon the myrtle-spray, which, after a moment's pause of astonishment, Viola kissed off, and then laid the graceful branch in her bosom.

After this moment the music of the pipe was again heard from the neighbouring trees; the strain was now more broken and quicker. A brilliant humming-bird shot from the forest, and hovered above the flowers of the Vase. None knew what to expect; but after several minutes all started and grasped at those beside them. The Vase itself was now changing its form. Amid the flowers appeared a human face: roses, red and white, bloomed on the cheeks; the lips were like a blown carnation; the rich brown hair hung in clusters on the neck, and was crowned with flowers; the alabaster sculpture itself disappeared; and the form expanded, and became that of a figure suitable to the lovely head. The vision appeared to move very gently to the sound of the music, and to be so slight that it might have risen into the air upon the evening breeze. Suddenly one of the ladies exclaimed, "It is Viola!" and Viola herself rose in amazement from the turf, and confronted her image. They were exactly similar, except that, when the setting sun shone on the neck and shoulder of the phantom, some of the spectators thought the flesh was slightly transparent.

Viola was determined not to be daunted by the effort of

power, to which she had challenged the Magician, and looked at the figure and smiled. The blooming face smiled too, and bent slightly towards her; and the lady could hardly refrain from murmuring, while she beheld the copy of herself, "How exquisite! How lovely!" With a swift impulse she stepped forward to touch the face with hers. The music made a loud and vehement turn; and, though to the bystanders it seemed that Viola kissed the mouth of Viola, the lips and face that were present to the eye and feeling of the maiden, became at the instant those of the Magician. She trembled and shrank back. The music from the thicket changed its tune and character, and became more irregular and plaintive. The magic form lost its animation; the flowers and the alabaster returned; and the Nymph and her thyrsus were fixed again in sculptured beauty.

Viola stepped close to the Vase, and leant her brow among the flowers on the brim, apparently sunk in reflection. The others expressed their wonder in hasty words and broken sentences; and, when they could turn and look quietly round, the Magician was again in their circle. Viola raised her head with a thoughtful smile, still resting her hand upon the Vase, and thanked him for his labour.

"But," said one of the party to him, "could you reverse the charm, and turn Viola into a vase?"

"That also I would endeavour to do, if I had her permission."

"You have it," she answered, "provided you will not leave me in that shape, beautiful as it is; for I am more accustomed to my own."

"No," he said, "if I may but approach the vase and touch it, I can answer for again accomplishing your transformation."

She nodded her assent cheerfully; and again he touched his instrument. He stood before her, and fixed his deep dark eyes on hers, which hardly sustained the look. To the thought of those around, the forms of both expanded and grew half luminous in the twilight. The music which he now produced, though not loud, was so keen and melting, that it passed through the very hearts and brains and limbs of all, and trembled in every fibre of their fingers. It swelled and complicated its volume, and seemed to grow upward from the pipe, and spin around like a huge pillar between earth and sky. And now it was heard to come, not merely from the instrument, but from the hands and head and whole figure of the player; and every hair of his long black locks gave forth a stream of melody. Viola was rooted to the ground, but shook and wavered like a tree in a strong wind. In a few seconds the breathing glowing maiden sank into a flower-crowned vase, as graceful and noble as the other, which it completely resembled. The Magician seemed exhausted by his efforts, and fell softly on the grass with his pipe beside him. One of Viola's friends whispered to her companions, "Now were it a jest to prevent him from approaching, and thus retain her for a time as she is."

All assented; and, forming a ring between the Magician and the transformed damsel, they danced laughing around, so as to make it impossible for him to approach. He gazed at them a moment, rose, and took water in his hand from a fountain near him, and scattered it over them. Instantly they sank in sleep on the green turf and the last dim ray of sunset fell on their repose. He then began to whisper music on his pipe, rather than to play it, drew near gently to the vase, and, gathering a sprig of myrtle from the garland, placed it next his heart. The lady swiftly emerged from her enchantment, and stood beside him in the clear night.

"Viola, can you forgive me?"

"For what transgression?" she enquired. "I have been but for a few moments in a dream."

"Was it a happy one?" said the Magician.

She cast down her eyes; and it was a moment before she replied; "Not painful. But what is your offence?"

"Have you not lost your myrtle?"

She felt for it, and blushed to find it missing. "Was it for this that you said it was necessary you should approach me, in order to restore me to my present form?"

He coloured, smiled, and said, "You have guessed well. But you have not yet granted me pardon."

She held out her hand; he pressed it to his lips; and she questioned him anew. "Tell me why you selected me for the object of your art, instead of calling some of your legion of phantoms out of nothing?"

"Have you," he replied, "no feeling in your heart, which makes you of greater importance to me than the fairest spirit that ever shot from a star to earth?" He paused for an instant; and, as she made no answer, he continued: "I could indeed have called a multitude of beings out of air, all exquisite, all different; but I could not have given any of them a human heart to love me; and you are the first I have found whom I could love, and having in yourself an answering affection."

"Will you not release our friends?" asked Viola.

"They will wake," said he, "at the rising of the moon."

When the moon rose they awoke; but Viola and the

Magician had departed from the Palace of Morgana. Their friends found lingering in their ears the fragments of a chant, which they imagined they must have heard during their sleep, and of which this was the purport:

> Into the world of life away!
> Away from the valley of pleasant dreams!
> Through change and sorrow we now shall stray,
> Where time no longer a sun-flash seems.
>
> Away from the garden of flowery joys,
> Where nothing was ended, and all began;
> From a land where spades and swords were toys,
> And nought was real enough for man.
>
> We shall struggle, and toil, and mourn;
> Our sky will often be dark above:
> But within us the flame of song shall burn;
> And still it will be our bliss to love.

A Chronicle of England

(From Blackwood's Magazine, 1840)

Hark! above the Sea of Things,
How the uncouth mermaid sings:
Wisdom's Pearl doth often dwell
Closed in Fancy's rainbow shell.

"Sister," said the little one to her companion, "dost thou remember aught of this fair bay, these soft white sands, and yonder woody rocks?"

"Nay," replied the other, who was somewhat taller, and with a fuller yet sweet voice, "I knew not that I had ever been here before. And yet it seems not altogether new, but like a vision seen in dreams. The sea ripples on the sand with a sound which I feel as friendly and not unknown. Those purple shapes that rise out of the distant blue, and float past over the surface like the shadows of clouds, do not fill me with the terror which haunts me when I look on vast and strange appearances."

"To me," said the little one, "they look only somewhat more distinct than the marks which I have so often watched upon the sea."

"Oh! far brighter are they in colour, far more peculiar and more various in their forms. My heart beats while I look at them. There are ships and horses, living figures, bearded, crowned, armed, and some bear banners and some books, and softer shapes, waving and glistening with plumes, veils, and garlands. Ah! now 'tis gone."

"Rightly art thou called the Daughter of the Sea, and art indeed our own Sea-Child. Here in this bay did I and my sisters, in this land of Faëry, first find our nursling of another race."

"Was this then my first name among you, beloved friends? The bay is so beautiful, that, even in your land of Faëry, I have seen no spot where it were better to open one's eyes upon the light."

"Yes, here did our Sea-Child first meet our gaze. I and a troop of my sisters were singing on the shore our ancient Song of Pearls, and watching the sun, which, while we sang, and while it went down, changed the sands its beams fell on into gold, and the foam that rippled to the shore into silver. We had often watched it before; and we knew that, if without ceasing our song we gathered the gold sands and silver foam while the sun was on them, into the shells that lay about, they would continue in their changed state. Left till sunset, they returned to what they were, and we had only the sands and foam. We thought the sport so pleasant, that we had carried it on for some minutes, and even amused ourselves with scattering the shining dust over each other's hair, when I saw something floating between us and the sun. We all looked; and soon it drifted near us, and was entangled in the web of sea-weed that waves in the tide round this black single rock. A large sea-eagle at the moment stooped to seize the prize. But I wished myself there before it; and one bound carried me farther than a long stone's-throw of our dark enemies the mountaineers. Thus the eagle in his descent struck only the waters with his talons, and flew off again screaming to the clouds, while I brought what I had won to my sisters."

"Dear one!" said the Sea-Child, "I guess what it was." And she kissed the airy face of her companion with her own, which seemed rather of rose-leaves, and the other only of coloured vapour.

"Yes," said she, "my own Sea-Child, there was a small basket of palm-leaf lined with the down of the phoenix; and in this the baby lay asleep. Beautiful it was indeed, but far unlike the beauty of my sisters. We cared no more for gold or silver dust, or rippling waves, or the rays of the setting sun. We even hushed our song, and bent over our nursling, and took her to be our own. Thus was it that our Sea-Child came to our Faëryland."

The Sea-Child bent to embrace her friend; for she was somewhat taller than the elfin sprite. They could not hold each other in their arms; for one was gleaming air, and the other human substance. But the fairy hung round the child, as the reflection of a figure in bright water round one who bathes at the same spot of the same transparent pool. To the phantom it was more delightful than to rest and breathe upon a bank of flowers: to the mortal it seemed as if she was encompassed by a soft warm air, full of the odours of opening carnations and of ripe fruits.

"Let us sit here," said the Sea-Child, "and look around us, and discourse."

She placed herself on a mossy stone at the foot of a green birch-tree; and the fairy sat on the extremity of one of the sprays, which hung beside her companion's face, and which hardly bent a hair's-breadth with her weight. By one hand she held to a leaf above her, and with the other touched the dark-brown locks that streamed round the mortal head. The child sat, and looked down, and seemed to think, till the fairy said, "Why art thou sad? Of what art thou musing?"

The child blushed, and stooped her head, and at last looked up confusedly and said: "I never before felt so strongly the difference between me and you, who call me sister. Here, while we sit together on the spot where I was first wafted to your hands, it seems to me strange, — so strange! — that ye should have adopted me for your own, and not thrown me back into the waters, or left me a prey to the mountaineers, from whom ye have so long protected me."

"Strange!" said the other, "how strange? We could do no otherwise than we did. I know not how it is, that our Sea-Child often speaks as if it were possible to do aught else than what one wishes. We felt we loved you: we saw that, in that pretty but solid mortal frame, there was a breath and beauty like our own, though also something akin to those huge enemies, who, but for our cunning, would swiftly have devoured thee."

"I too never thought of it in former years; but now, when I believe I am really capable of loving you, when I more want to be loved, and to find nothing dividing me from you, it seems so unnatural, so horrible, that I should be altogether unlike you. You are all of sunbeams and bright hues, and are soft like dewy gossamers; and I, — my limbs, through which no ray can pass, my head, that crushes the flowers I rest it on, as if it had been a head carved in stone! — Oh, sister! I am wretched at the thought. I touched the wing of a butterfly only yesterday with my finger; and I could perceive it shrink and shiver with pain. My touch had bruised its wing; and I thought I could see it ache, as it flew frightened away."

She burst into tears; and these were the first that ever were shed in Faëryland. But there they could not flow long; and she soon shook them from her eyes, and looked up smiling and said: "There thou see'st, dear sister, how unfit I am to live with such as thee. Better perhaps had I met my natural fate, and been destroyed on my first arrival by thy monstrous foes, or by the eagle from which thou didst save me."

"Strange would it have been, if we had not had wit enough to disappoint that big, brutal race!"

"I never could well understand why it was that they hated either you or me."

"They could not do otherwise being what they are, — thou what thou art, — and we the sprites thou knowest us. Curious is the tale, and long to tell, of all that has happened betwixt them and us."

"How came ye to have such dreadful inhabitants in your isle of Faëry?"

"Ah! that I know not. They and we seem to belong to it by the same necessity. Before thou camest we had no measure of time; which we now reckon, as thou knowest, by thy years, not by ours. Till then our existence was like what thou describest thy dreams to be. It is in watching thee, that we have learned to mark how thy fancies and wishes and actions rise and succeed one another, as the sun and moon, the stars and clouds travel and change. And even now I hardly feel, as thou appearest to do, what is meant by to-day, yesterday, and to-morrow. Of times and years therefore I can tell thee little. We grow not old, nor cease to be young. Nor can we say of each other, as we can of thee, — thou art such a one, and none else. We discern differences of sunshine and shade, of land and sea, of wind and calm; but all of us feel alike under the same circumstances, and have no fixed peculiarity of being, such as that which makes thee so different from us. I know not whether it was I, or some other of my sisters, who visited this field and shore yesterday, and the day before danced in the showering drops of the white waterfall yonder up the valley. Each of us feels as all do, and all as each. I love thee not more than do my sisters, nor they more than I. Of our past life I only know, that we seemed always to have been in this our own land, and to have been happy here. The flowers fill us with odours, the sky with warmth; the dews bathe us in delight; the moonbeams wind us in a ring with filmy threads when we dance upon the sands; and, when the woods murmur above us, we have a thrill of quiet joy, which belongs not to me more than to another, but is the common bliss of all. Of all times have the mountains and deep ravines and bare and rocky uplands of our isle been the abode of a fierce and ugly race of giants, whom we have been accustomed to call our brothers, and to believe them allied with us by nature, though between us there has ever been a mortal enmity."

"Often, often," said the Sea-Child, "have I thought how much happier we should be, had there been no giants in the land."

"I know not," replied the fairy, "how that might be. Much is the vexation that they cause us; but it is said that our race is inseparable from theirs, and that, if they were altogether destroyed, we also must perish. Never, till we had thee among us, did their enmity seem very dangerous, difficult as it often was to avoid their injuries. Always, as now, when the shadows of the storm-cloud swept from the hills over our plains, when the dark mist rolled out of the ravines down to our sunny meadows, the shaggy and huge creatures strode forth from their caves and forests, leaning on their pine clubs, shouting and growling, defacing our green and flowery sward with their weighty tramp, and scaring us away before them. When, as it has happened, some of us were trodden beneath their feet, or dashed below their swinging clubs, a faint shriek, a sudden blaze burst from under the blow; and all of us, lurking beneath the waterfalls, clinging amid the hidden nooks of flowers, or shrunken into sparry grottoes in the rocks, felt stricken and agonized, although none of us could cease to live. All round this bay, and others larger and more broken of our shore, the giant horde of our brothers would sit upon the cliffs and crags, looking themselves like prodigious rocks, and, with the rain and storm about them, and the sea-foam dashing up against their knees, would wash their dark beards in the brine, and seem to laugh aloud at the sound of the tempest. But when calm and sunshine were about to return, they always sprang from their places on the shore, and, like one of those herds of wild bulls that they chase before them, hurried back with dizzy bellowings, and rush of limbs and clubs, into their dark mountains. Sometimes indeed they were more malicious, and sought more resolutely to do us mischief. I have known them tear asunder the jaws of one of their hill-torrents, so as to pour the waters suddenly on our fields and valleys. Sometimes too we have seen them standing upon the mountains, with their figures marked against the sky, plying great stems of trees around a mass of snow and ice, till, loosened at last, it rolled down mile after mile, crashing through wood and stream. Thus our warm bright haunts were buried under a frozen heap of ruins, while the laughter of the mountain-monsters rang through the air, above the roar of the falling mass. But often we had our revenge. Once, when the storms had gathered fiercely on those far hills, and rushed in rainy gusts and black fogs down every gully, and opened at last over the green vale and sunny bay, our brothers hurried in tumult from their own region, their swinish ears tossing in the dark folds of their locks and beards, and, with mouths like wolves, drinking in the tempest as they ran. They rioted and triumphed on the shore, while the wind whistled loudly round them; and they played with the billows which tumbled on the beach, as I have seen you play with lambs in the green fields. We peeped from the grottoes where we had hidden ourselves, and saw them catch some round black heaps out of the waters, like skins of animals full of liquid. These they threw at each other, till at last one burst, and covered the giant whom it had struck with a red stain. On this there was a loud shout: they flung the skins about no more, but caught them tenderly in their arms, lifted them to their mouths, bit them open and drained the contents. This increased their tumult and grim joy; and they turned to the meadow, and began to wrestle and leap and tear down the young trees, and disport themselves, till one by one they sank upon the turf in sleep. The storm was clearing off: we ventured from our hiding-places, and looked upon the hairy dismal shapes, that lay scattered and heaped like brown rocks overgrown with weeds and moss. Suddenly we all looked at each other, and determined what to do. We pierced through the crevices of our grottoes, till we reached a fount of sunny fire.

This we drew upwards by our singing to follow us, and led it in a channel over the grass, till it formed a stream of diamond light, dividing this field from the mountains, and encircling the whole host of giants. The warm sunshine at the same time began to play on them. They felt the soft sweet flowery air of our lower land; our songs sounded in their bristled ears; and they began to toss, roll, snort, and endeavoured to rise and escape to their dark hills. But this was not so easy now. They could not pass the bright pure stream. The sunshine, in which we revelled, weakened them so much that they could not rise and stand, but staggered on their knees, fell upon their hands and faces, and seemed to dissolve away, like their own ice-crags when flung with all their clay and withered herbage down into our warm lakes and dells. We thought there was now a chance of seeing our enemies, who were also our brothers, for ever destroyed. We began to deliberate whether we also should necessarily perish with them, when we heard a sudden gust of wind and flash of rain; another storm broke from the mountains; a torrent of snow-water quenched our diamond flame. The giants stood up, bold, wild, and strong as ever, leaped, roared, and swung their clubs, and, with the friendly tempest playing round them, stormed back into the depths of their own mountain world."

"Could ye not," said the Sea-Child, "have always taken refuge from them in the lower garden, where I have been with you?"

"We did not know it till thou wert among us, and should perhaps never have ventured thither, had we not been driven to distress by the hatred of the giants for thee. When we had thee for our nursling and sister, their attempts were no longer bursts of violence that passed away. They seemed always lying in wait to discover and to destroy thee. Had we not known a strain of music, of power when sung to frighten them away, thou, dear Sea-Child, wouldst long ere this have been taken from us. When they came rushing down in the wind and darkness, and sought for thee in every thicket, and every hollow tree, and under each of those large pink shells which we often made thy bed, they sang and shouted together such words as these:

> Lump and thump, and rattling clatter,
> These the brawny brothers love;
> While the lightnings flash and shatter,
> While the winds the forest tatter,
> We too spatter, stamp, and batter,
> Whirling our clubs at whate'er's above.

But we too had our song; and never could these grim wild beasts resist the spell, when we sang together with soft voice,

> The giant is strong; but the fairy is wise:
> And the clouds cannot wither the stars in the skies.

"Oh! well I remember," said her companion, "with what delight I first heard you sing that song. I fancied that, if I could only listen long enough to it, I should become as airy and gentle as ye are, and no longer be encumbered with this dark solid flesh. We were in that green chamber in the midst of red rocks, where the pines spread over the brinks of the precipices far above the mossy floor we sat on; and the vines hung their branches down the stony walls from the pine-boughs which they cling to on the summit, and drop their clusters into the smooth stream, with its floating water-lilies, which traverses the spot. There, dear sisters, were ye sporting, climbing up the vine-trails, and throwing yourselves headlong down, or lanching over the quick ripples of the stream. Ye had laid me on a bed of harebells; and I looked up with half-shut eyes. I saw your sparkling hosts pass to and fro up the cliff, through the straggling beams of sunshine; when something blacker than the pine-boughs on the summit appeared in the deepest of their shade. Long tangled locks, and two fierce round eyes, and a mouth with huge protruding lip, came on and peered over, till the monster spied me, and gave a yell. I saw a crag, with two young pine-trees growing on it, toppling before the thrust of his hand, and at the moment of falling to crush me. Then suddenly came your cry and song. A sheet of water, thinner than a rose-leaf, and transparent as the starry sky, rose from the stream, and seemed to form an arch above me. There was in it a perpetual trembling and eddying of the brightest colours; and I saw the forms of thousands of my sisters, floating, circling, wavering up and down in the liquid light. All seemed joining in the song, —

> The giant is strong; but the fairy is wise:
> And the clouds cannot wither the stars in the
> skies.

The crag fell, but shattered not my crystal vault, down the side of which it rolled into the stream; and the giant, with a roar of rage, fell after it, and stung by the warm air, and pierced through and through by the music, and writhing in the bright stream, half melted, half was broken like a lump of ice, and darkened the water, while he flowed away in it.”

“It was the frequency of such attempts however,” said the fairy, “which drove us to take refuge in the regions of our friends, the dwarfs. We found too that we had no longer the mere risk of being surprised by our enemies in the sudden descent of storm and mists, and through the opportunities of thick and gloomy lurking-places near our sunlit haunts. They had discovered a secret, by which they could at will darken and deface our whole kingdom, and blight all its sweet flowers and fruitage. There is somewhere, in the centre of their mountains, in the midst of desolate rocks, a black ravine. The upper end of it is enclosed by an enormous crag, which turns as on a pivot, and is the door of an immeasurable cave. The giants, hating our Sea-Child, and determined to drive her from the land, heaved with their pine-stem clubs at this great block of stone, until they had forced it open. Thence, so long as they had strength to hold it thus, a thick and chilling mist boiled out, poured down the glens and mountains, and stifled all our island. When they were so wearied with the huge weight that they could endure no longer, the rock swung to again and closed the opening; but not until the work was done for that time, and the land made wellnigh uninhabitable to thee and us. Then in the fearful gloom the giants rushed abroad, howling and trampling over high and low; and many were the devices we were compelled to use in order to preserve thee from their fury. We scattered the golden sea-sand, which had been transmuted by the sunbeams, over the softest greensward, and watered it with the dew shaken from musk-roses; and it grew up into a golden trelliswork, with large twining leaves of embossed gold, and fruits like bunches of stars. When thou hadst been sprinkled with the same dew, and so hushed into charmed sleep, we laid thee beneath the bowery roof, and kept watch around thee. The giants could not approach this spot; for it threw off the darkness, and burnt in the midst of storm and fog with an incessant light. But still we were obliged to be perpetually on our guard; and we shivered and pined in the desolation of our beautiful empire. At last we resolved to try our fortunes in a new region. When we had lulled thee into deep slumber, we all glided down the waterfall that pours out of the lake of lilies, and sank with it deep into the ground. We were here in the kingdom of the dwarfs.

"The little people showed us as much friendship, as the giants had ever displayed of enmity. Their great hall had a thousand columns, each of a different metal, and with a capital of a different precious stone. The roof was opal, and the floor lapis-lazuli. In the centre stood a pillar, which seemed cut off at half its height. On it sat a dwarf, rather smaller than the others, but broad and strong. His dark and twisted face looked like a little copy of one of the giants; but his clear blue eyes were as beautiful as ours, or as thine, my Sea-Child. He sat with his arms folded, and his legs hung down and swinging. His head was turned to one side, and rather upwards; and on the tip of his nose spun perpetually a little golden circle, with a golden pin run through it, on which it seemed to dance unweariedly, turning round and round for ever, smooth and swift as an eddy in a stream. In its whirl the little circle gave out large flakes of white fire, which formed a wheel of widening rings above the head of the dwarf, flashing off on all sides between the capitals of the pillars, and lighting the whole hall. The queer cunning look, with which the dwarf's blue eyes glanced up at the small spinner, as if it were alive, and answering his glances with its own, amused us much.

"The dwarfs, when we entered, were all placed round on ranges of seats rising above one another. Every seat was like a small pile of round plates of gold, each of them, as we afterwards found, having a head on it with some strange figures. These plates, the dwarfs told us, were all talismans, which would one day make the owners lords of the world. At the head of the hall, under a canopy of state, sat the king of the dwarfs, who looked wonderfully old and wise, with two eyes of ruby, and a long crystal tooth growing out of one side of his mouth, and a beard of gold-wire falling below his feet and twirled on the floor, going three times round the throne.

"'What seek ye?' said the King; and his words did not come out of his lips, but from a little hole in the top of his crystal tooth.

"'Help! necromancer.'

"'It belongeth rightly to the helpful, and shall not be denied you. What bring ye?'

"'A young Sea-Child.'

"'It is in the youngest that the oldest may see hope. She is welcome. What fear ye?'

"'The rage of the tall giants.'

"'We are deeper than they are high. I can protect you against them.'

"He rose up and walked before us; and his golden beard streamed behind over both his shoulders, and seemed to be a stately cloth woven with figures for us to walk on. There was darkness round us; and we advanced upon this shining path, following the dwarf, till suddenly he disappeared, and we found ourselves in the garden which thou hast dwelt in with us. Thou rememberest the still and glistening loveliness of the place; and of the moon that lighted it, and the sweet moonflowers that filled its glades, I need not speak. But thou knowest not what wise instruction the old dwarf king was wont to give us, while thou wert sleeping under the myrtle shade.

"'Mourn not,' he would say, 'fair sisters, that ye are driven from your upper land of life into this lower garden of peace.

"'All things are but as they must be; and, were they otherwise, they would not be the things they are.

"'Each worketh for itself, and doeth and knoweth all it can, save in so far as other things oppose it, which are also accomplishing their due tasks.

"'Each is but a portion of the whole, and vainly seeketh to be aught but that which the whole willeth it to be.

"'All, — that is, dwarfs, and giants, and fairies, and the world that holds them, — subsist in successions of strife, and, while they seem struggling to destroy each other, exert, as alone it is possible for them to do, the energies of their own being.

"'All rise out of death to life; and many are the semblances of death which still accompany their life at its highest. They grow into harmony only by discord with themselves and others, and, while they labour to escape the common lot, rebound painfully from the walls which they strive against idly.

"'The giant disturbeth, the fairy brighteneth, the dwarf enricheth the world. Each doeth well in his own work. But therein often must he thwart and cross the work of another.

"'I am oldest, I am wisest of workers in the world. I was at the birth of things; and what hath been I know well: but what is future I know not yet, nor can read whether there shall be a new birth of all that may bring death to me.'

"Thus did the old King teach us a sad yet melodious contentment, that seemed suited to that visionary garden. This quiet state however was not to last, nor the wisdom of the dwarfs to secure them happiness. We longed for our upper world of daylight and freedom; and thou seemedst rather dreaming than awake. Yet thou beamedst ever fairer and fairer, and didst grow in stature and in loveliness. Thus was it that thou wert the occasion of our first difference with the dwarfs. Their King, so old, so wise, looked on thee ever with more joy and sadness; and at last he told us that he would fain have thee for his queen, to abide with him always in that secret lunar empire. Us too the other dwarfs appeared to love more than we wished; and we found that we must either leave their dominions, or consent to inhabit them for ever. We spake to the old King, and said, that for thee it would be a woful doom to see our native Faëryland no more; and we entreated him of his goodness and wisdom to enable us to dwell there without further peril. Ruby tears fell from his ruby eyes upon his golden beard as he turned away; and the faces of all Dwarfland were darkened.

"No long space seemed to have passed, before we were summoned again to the great hall, while thou wert left sleeping in the moon-garden. The King was on his throne; the dwarfs were seated round. But, instead of the pillars we had seen before, the metals now had all become transparent; and in the midst of each stood one of our enemies, the giants, with one heavy hand hung down, and clenched, as if in pain, and the other raised above his head, and sustaining the capital of the column. The small gold plate with its gold pin still spun incessantly on the nose; the blue eyes still watched it cunningly; the flakes of fire streamed off and flew between the pillars, and scorched the faces and brown-red shoulders of the giants. Our enemies grinned and writhed when they saw us, but seemed unable to utter any sound. The dwarfs also did not speak; but the King rose and moved before us. His beard fell over his shoulders, and formed a path on which we walked. We proceeded on and on, till the Dwarfland seemed changing, and daylight fell faintly upon us. The King grew more and more like the stones and trees around; and at last, we knew not how, instead of his figure before us, there was only a cleft in the rock, nearly of the same shape. The golden beard was now a track of golden sands, such as we had often seen before, with the bright sunshine falling on it. We were again in our own world of Faery. But oh, dear Sea-Child! I cannot say the grief that smote us when we missed thee. We wailed and drooped; and even the delights of our land could do nothing to console us, till we found thee sleeping in a grotto of diamond and emerald, which recalled the treasures of the dwarfs to us. Even now we were not happy; for we remembered a prophecy of the old man, that, though he might restore us to our home, and rescue us from the giants, short would be our enjoyment of thee whom we had refused him."

The companions embraced anew; and the fairy hung round her friend like a rainbow on a smooth green hill. The fairies now poured in on all sides, singing and exulting in their own land, though not without a thought of grief from the dwarf's prophecy. The sun was hanging over the sea, and gilding the shore; and they looked at the bright waters, and marked the spot where they had first discerned the Sea-Child's swimming cradle. Lo! there was again a speck. A floating shape appeared, and came nearer and nearer. It looked a living thing. Soon it touched the shore; and they saw a figure like that of the Sea-Child, but taller and stronger and bolder, and in a stately dress. The fairies said in their hearts, It is a man! Them he seemed not to see, but only her. She was frightened, but with a mixture of gladness at his appearance, and was trembling and nigh to sink, when he took her in his arms, and spake to her of hope and joy.

"I am come from distant lands upon this strange adventure, warned in dreams, and by aerial voices, and by ancient lays, that here I should find my bride, and the queen of my new dominions."

He too was beautiful, and of a sweet voice; and she heard him with more fear than pain. When she looked around, she no longer saw the fairies near. There were gleams floating over the landscape, and quivering in the woods, and a song of sweet sorrow, so sweet, that, as it died away, it left the sense of an eternal peace.

Thus did the land of England receive its first inhabitants. Ever since has it been favoured by the fairies; the dwarfs have enriched it secretly; and the giants have upborne its foundations upon their hands, and done it huge though sullen service.

The Suit of Armour and the Skeleton

(From Blackwood's Magazine, 1838)

Armour. At last it is night, still night! The crowd, who thronged the church during the day, and gazed at me as a toy for their idleness, are gone; and I am alone. Ah! I cannot weep; but it is a comfort to sigh, to speak. There are none to hear. The princely warriors who fought around me, are all with him who wore me, dead, — perished, with the eyes that were wont to admire me; and I am alone in the world. Ah!

Skeleton. Is it from yonder rusty armour that the voice comes? If so, I pray thee tell me how it befalls that thou hast the power of speech?

Armour. I know not what thou art that askest; but I will answer thee. The magic of the gnomes, whom he that framed me called to his aid, gave me this mournful privilege. On this one night during the year I wake to consciousness and speech; and now my hour is come. But do thou in turn tell me what thou art.

Skeleton. I am the skeleton in the niche over against thee. This is the eve of the festival of St. John, to whose honour I, or rather he that animated me, was especially devoted; and it is my destiny, for the years that must pass before I can entirely rest, to tingle on this one night with life, and listen, and speak. Wilt thou inform me what are the sorrows which thou so sorely bewailest?

Armour. Nay, tell me first, how it comes to pass that now for the first time I hear thee, though I have held my present place for fifty years?

Skeleton. I have been transferred hither but a few days since, as the precious relics of a saint, and, clad in a monastic garb, am fixed in a shrine close to that marble tomb over which thou so grimly standest. Many miracles, of which I know nothing, are said to have attended my removal hither; for men, till they learn to wonder at and love truth, will exercise themselves in wondering at falsehood and loving it.

Armour. Thou art then, after all, but the skeleton of some poor devout peasant. I am the armour of a Duke, and converse not on equal terms with such as thee.

Skeleton. Despise not what thou hast not well understood and seen through; a precept which I suspect would much lessen the range of thy contempt. On equal terms indeed we converse not; for I was once alive; and thou, — what art thou? a mass of steel and gold, framed for another's use, and in thyself but some few jots better than nothing.

Armour. I had power by my aspect, to daunt many hearts in bosoms such as thine, and to protect one with which thou durst not have claimed kindred.

Skeleton. Where is that one now?

Armour. To thy thought it may be only dust. But it lives for ever in story, as the heart of a wise, brave, and courteous knight and ruler.

Skeleton. It lives in story? Ay, so do the miracles they say I wrought on being removed hither.

Armour. Churl! Be gone, or be silent! Thou knowest well that thy proper place, whence thou hast been so ignorantly lifted, is many a lance's length from me.

Skeleton. Friend, be not wrath. Thy place would perhaps be, perhaps will be, a blacksmith's forge, where thou wilt be hammered into sickles for reapers, and shoes for pack-horses.

Armour. Peace, scoffer! I will not answer thy base ribaldry. And yet, peasant that thou art, thou speakest but as thou must needs think. I will discourse with thee on other matters; for so seldom comes the gift of speech, even to me, noble and time-honoured as I am, that it must not be suppressed; and there is none but thou to hear. Strange destiny! I that have blazed in the courts of kings, and been the morning-star of battles, am now lonely, empty, dimmed with dust, and must sigh over all that has been, and all that is, and be heard only by a thing like this. O royal days of courtesy and valour! O fervid life of enterprise and joy! how are ye buried under the slabs and tombs, and the clay of battle-fields; and I alone remain, to waste and sadden in a withered and dead world.

Skeleton. Dost thou then think, because thou art laid aside as a vain memorial, that all things else are rusted and abandoned? that the stars are clogged and ceasing in their courses, and the earth drying up and failing, because thy joints move no more, and thy vainer idea has waned into a shred? Dost thou fancy that mankind are now lifeless images fixed to a wall, or that all succeeding generations must pine and perish on the tomb of thy former wearer?

Armour. I will not answer thy ill-advised question, but in turn will enquire of thee: Dost thou not perceive what melancholy aspects of decay fill this old and stately building, — how sadly, through these pale-faced, richly-vested shadows in the coloured windows, the moon-beams glance, — how dark and spectral these vaults of the roof above, — with how many epitaphs of death and weary knees of penitents that pavement is worn away, — how these pillars and buttresses stand like over-tired penal giants? The bells seem meant to utter nothing but a knell; and, when they ring more cheerfully, it is a mad helpless merriment. The voices of the priests sound like a witch's croak over her wretched sorcery. The people, who frequent these aisles and chapels, look and move as if they were a train of spectres trying to persuade themselves that in their religious offices is a respite for their doom in truth long since accomplished. The world which I see and hear of, is all a tomb full of dust and darkness; and what passes for life is but the nightmare-dream ruling over the endless sleep of death.

Skeleton. Thee, my friend, a nightmare must possess; else couldst thou not be thus deluded. Thy hour indeed of dignity and pomp has passed away, as the hour will doubtless pass of the hills and rocks, nay, even of the stars. These, like thee, will pass into new forms of being; but whatever is worth preserving, will assuredly remain and be immortal. Nothing that we know of is outwardly indestructible; but nothing is destitute of some principle within it that cannot perish. All no doubt, that has been thrust out of its place into some unsuitable elevation, will hereafter sink, while all that has been unduly depressed will rise. But to waste words in lamenting over this righteous law, becomes only, — excuse my abruptness, — an empty head, or emptier iron head-piece.

Armour. Poor heap of dryness and desolation! In thy hollow bones and heartless ribs what life plays? Indeed I am void and aimless; but I know myself and my own misery. I am like all of fairest and best that is. I have been visited and filled and lifted up for a season, by a power that seemed to be great and lasting. It has passed away, and left me a relic of what once I was, or was imagined to be. So is it with all things. All are but wrecks and memorials of delusions, that once were bright, and now have vanished. Mythologies, and the sweet dreams of poets, and the flushing fancies of youthful hearts, heroic histories, and devout religions, all play their summer meteors across the sky for a moment, and then leave a deeper than the first blackness. So too the clouds that catch a rosy morning tinge, float away into mist and storm, and bequeath to the vapours of a new day the gaudy task of cheating men's eyes with new images of worthless beauty. The mountains, above which they hover, seem to stand fast, but are for ever wearing down into the clay and ruins, which their torrents carry to the sea. Cities and kingdoms are built up like rainbows, so to vanish; and the old oak, beneath which laws have been made and treaties sworn for centuries, is blown down and used for firewood, to burn the statutes and leagues which it seemed to consecrate. Say no more. He who has seen the hard haggard old man stand between his own grave and the cradle of his grandchild, and watch the stormy wrinkles grow wet with tears at the thought of all the infant will first believe in and then unlearn, — he knows enough of existence. After all thy years, only folly such as thine could dream of aught other than despair.

Skeleton. The old man weeps, because he no longer enjoys his hopes as formerly, not because he no longer possesses them. That he can mourn over their faded colouring, obscure perhaps only to obscure eyes, shows how clear their forms and undying lineaments still are to his heart. Were it otherwise, were his existence devoid of all hope, he would not weep: he would sink down at once into a heap of clay, not such as the sexton buries, which still bears witness of what it has enfolded, but such as that which he turns up with his shovel, and again with his shovel replaces. When that hour of burial comes, hymns and prayers and reverential thoughts and looks attest how solemn and precious to man, how far from empty and insignificant, is all that has ever borne the aspect of a man, and been called by a man's name. Men deal with mere lies as what they are, and cast away to rot their worn-out gloves and tattered masks and cowls. But because they know their lives are not lies, not insane fancies, or mere slimy bubbles, they treat with holy regard and piety whatever their lives have animated, even though it be a hideous corpse.

Armour. Speak as thou wilt out of thy school-primer, even thou wilt hardly say, that, amid these aisles and tombs and priestly mummeries, thy existence is serene and joyous. What then must mine be? For I have always, brooding in my hollow darkness, the remembrance of what I once was, and of all that then surrounded me. Whatever has been beautiful and majestic on earth, appears to me a train, such as I once headed, of princely panoplies, with plumes mighty as the wings of eagles, and banners fit to gather and impassion kingdoms. Taller and stronger and far fairer than the crowd of men, whom they sway and dazzle, they move over the ground in morning light to the measures of trumpet-music; and earth sounds proudlier at their tread. Heroes, kings, and gods, — valour, courtesy, wisdom, eloquence, what are they all but mailed and radiant images, that march over the world and pass away into darkness? Mankind indeed remain; but they are a heap of strewn and withered leaves, torn from the stately branches on which they once grew. Even now, methinks, could I open to thee a way below these charnel-vaults, we might at last emerge into a rocky plain, lighted only by the clear moon, and behold, seated on their marble chairs, the gold and steel and bronze figures, gigantic, silent, awful with severe immortal pride, and exempt from pain or decay. But alas! if, as I would fain believe, these anywhere exist, it is in a world apart and of their own. They have been seen for some scanty hours by a race too mean for them, have founded kingdoms, freed or conquered nations, — as momentary sunbright apparitions have turned battles, or quelled the fears of wavering councils by one pealing utterance of disdain. But they are gone for ever. This earth could not detain them; for it was not worthy of them; and now nothing remains but to groan, and, when groans are spent, be silent.

Skeleton. Thou at least seemest to find a better use for thy iron lips than merely groaning. Thy words sound as if thou hadst a pleasure in being listened to, which thy vanity, aping pride, leads thee to disclaim. But be it so. I am well pleased that thou art more humane and kindly than thou pretendest; and I can forgive the boyish folly of thy affected haughty indifference.

Armour. Were I not nailed here, like Prometheus to his rock, I would soon avenge thy insults.

Skeleton. Wert thou not nailed there, like a kite on a barn-door, thou wouldst not have been rhapsodizing thy sickly fancies for the last half-hour. Nor in that case should

I have been thinking what insane mouthing quackeries one may persuade oneself, and fancy one persuades others, are the strains of a peculiar and supreme wisdom. Permit me therefore to observe, that all you have been saying is, as might have been expected, mere worthless absurdity, a thumping together of fine words, in hopes that some of them may stick to each other, and fit, and so turn out intelligible. The amount of meaning is about equal to that of thread in the hastily stitched tawdry patchwork of a masquerade dress, and barely serves the same purpose of seeming to hold together the ill-assorted scraps and glaring colours. Yet a thread of meaning there is; and on this let me hang some words of answer. Do you in truth fancy that the life of the human race, of which one slight impulse is now strangely lingering in your frame and mind, exists only to produce some few enormous glittering shapes of strength and subtlety? Or are not men, even the meanest and most wretched, could we look into them, and read their whole story and destination, all the true-born children of the infinite One, and each, more or less, a conscious image of the great whole, and of Him whom it visibly reflects? Who dares say that life is given to spend itself in those blazing bursts, and amid those stormy quivering peaks, which alone thou pretendest to honour? In the millions of dark huts, and among the countless daily sordid cares of all generations, Heaven works unseen beneath, and bends above; and man is in himself greater than all the outward liveries in which he can clothe his lot. Often, how often! he makes himself little, in striving to be falsely great. He lays waste the garden, in which he might live a free demigod, and shovels and piles the soil into a tomb-like pyramid, to stand on its narrow peak alone, an imprisoned, idle, ape-like dwarf. And what is true of man, is true of all things and powers. In its right place, and for its true purpose, everything is good, precious, holy. Only let all lies be boldly unsaid, and faithfully suffered for, — all perversions, even at the cost of much writhing, be patiently turned inside out, and so restored to their true state. Courage, friend, courage! After sufficient wasting and hammering, thou thyself mayst come at last to be an honest serviceable ploughshare.

Armour. Rather, ten thousand times rather, would I sink into utter nothingness.

Skeleton. Pshaw! I have an ear for music and rational discourse, but none for the clang and clatter of old iron, unless indeed it helped to make the bees swarm. The sense too of a simmering-pot, or of the sound of an axe, I can understand. But when I see anything that strives to be more than it can be, I know there is something that will soon become less than it is. We may however know more of each other, and of the truth in these matters, if thou wilt tell me some chief passages from the history of him whose tomb thou adornest.

Armour. That will I do right willingly; and so shalt thou see and own how vain and ill-considered thy scoffs have been. Duke Eberhard, whose effigy lies below me carved in stone, with an eagle on his helmet, and a bear at his feet, was the lord of five great castles; and three hundred knights followed him to battle. Never pilgrim passed his gates, without receiving a meal of venison, and a draught of wine from a golden cup. Never minstrel sang in his hall, and wanted the guerdon of four golden pieces, and a mantle edged with fur. The burghers of twelve towns did homage to him; and from each town he yearly received twelve casks of wine and a golden chain. The man was bold who dared do aught but bless Duke Eberhard within three long days' ride of the borders of his land. Noble horses of Flanders, brave armours from Italy, keen dogs, fair hawks, many a sweet-voiced minstrel, and a storming train of riders were gathered daily round the Duke; and he himself was of all the stateliest sight to see. One town there was within the circuit of his domains, that ever refused to yield him homage. Its minstrels sang no songs in his honour; and its burghers rendered him neither casks of wine nor golden chains, but rather cold looks and haughty pretensions, talking of I know not what old privileges and claims to freedom. Nay, when, to do them honour, arrayed in steel, and followed by fifty knights and all their squires and pages, he approached their walls to brighten their high feast with his presence, they closed the gates against him. A crack-voiced harper on a tower drawled a scurvy ballad in mockery, as the Duke in high wrath turned bridle, and, biting his lip, and shaking his plumed head, rode back ten leagues from the gates of Rothburg to his castle of Falkesheim. Now thou must know that the Duke of Bavaria's daughter had chosen Eberhard for her champion when he jousted at Augsburg; and she was the fairest woman, save one peasant girl, I ever looked upon. But she would not give him any token of her favour to wear, till he should be able to show it on entering the gates of that rebellious town. Judge then of my noble master's rightful anger, when these base burghers opposed his sovereign will, and darkened the smiles of so admirable a lady. Not long could their insolence avail. He sent squires, pilgrims, minstrels, merchants of his followers into the city, with store of gold and jewels. More than one rosy-cheeked and bright-eyed damsel of France and Italy were found to do his bidding, and win the younger burghers to his will. The chief of all these sullen citizens was an old, hard-browed, stiff-necked man, to whom wealth and pleasure were as dew-drops on a rock. Him five knights lay in wait for near the walls. They sent to tell him that a palmer, who brought news of his only son from beyond the seas, was under a vow not to enter any town, and waited for him at the edge of the forest. The lure succeeded; and ere morning he was hanging, forty feet high, on a pine-tree before the drawbridge of Falkesheim. Courage and policy and a liberal hand soon taught the citizens in whose power lay true honour and lasting safety; and a solemn deputation came to the castle to entreat my Lord that of his great goodness he would receive the fealty of his poor servants. He was pleased to be entreated, and smiled on them graciously, nothing reproaching them with their former manifold arrogances. On the third day after, the Duke, clad in the complete mail that now hangs over his tomb, and wearing on his arm the scarf of the Lady Matilda of Bavaria, entered, at the head of his retainers, the gate from which he had been driven with shame but eight months before. The train of Barons and Knights that followed him would have befitted the Emperor; and of the armours which flashed affright that day into the eyes of the ignorant and rascal citizens, was none so rich and perfect as that of Duke Eberhard. At the high feast which celebrated his entry, ten minstrels sang his praises from the gallery of the hall, on each of whom the town was fain to bestow great largess. The railer who had once jeered from their walls was led by them, — for so the Duke required, — before the dais, with his hands tied behind him, and was then scourged by the grooms beyond the gates, and his harp broken and cast into the river. Of many goodly solemnities which I might recount, this one was, methinks, for a chivalrous and loyal spirit, the sweetest and most joyous. Every nobly born guest was gay and festal; and it added to the pleasure of all to see the sad and writhing looks of the cowed citizens. Canst thou wonder that, when I think of these things, and of him who now lies in dust below, I say the world has but sparkled up for some rare moments into a generous flame, and is now sunk for ever into mouldering dismal darkness? O Eberhard! how little could the crowd of mortals comprehend thy mighty and indomitable soul, ever swelling to embrace a larger compass of action and glory, ever looking with a stern and just disdain on the meaner throng that pressed like emmets round thy strong gigantic footsteps!

Skeleton. Dost thou remember the name of the peasant girl whose beauty thou spakest of?

Armour. If I remember, she was called Agnes. But why askest thou? Didst thou know aught of her?

Skeleton. There was a maiden of that name, daughter to a poor labourer, his only child, and without a mother. A great Lord, on whose domains they lived, cast on her the eyes of unlawful affection, when she was still almost a child. Ere long he commanded her father to send her to his castle, that she might attend on the wife of one of his Squires; for he was himself unmarried. It was well known what household he kept, and what mind was his towards the beautiful woman that approached his path. So her father refused the honour designed for him. Next day a man-at-arms, riding along the road close by the field where he wrought, shot at him, as if in sport, with his cross-bow, and sent the bolt through his arm. He knew that he dared no longer abide there; and at nightfall he left his cottage, and fled with his daughter into the heart of the forest, where he lived under the trees till he could build himself a hut of branches. Here they dwelt for many weeks; and the fair girl never murmured at her lot, but was peaceful and joyous to be with her father, and to do his will. Sometimes at night he returned to his former village, many leagues away, and obtained some help of food and clothing from his neighbours. On one of these occasions he was seen by some of the foresters, pursued, and led before the Lord, who commanded him to discover the retreat of his runaway vassal, his daughter. He refused, and was cast into a prison below the castle, which looked out from the rock over the plain and river, and from which he could see his native village and his former home. Here for weeks he lay without tidings of his child, and could only gaze at the dark edge of the forest in which he had left her, or look away to the deserted cottage where she had been born, and where he had lived with her mother. He never heard the horn blown, and the tramp and clash of the hunting train, and saw them wind down the hill and cross the river to hunt in the woods, but it seemed to him that they must needs find a human prey, for which they sought not. At last his fears came true. He heard the varied cries, and the shouts, and the baying of dogs, and all the tumult of the returning chase; and soon a young girl ran faltering from amid the trees, and hurried towards the well-known cottage. A moment after, the Duke appeared on horseback with many riders around him. Guiding the pursuit, he sent them in different directions, and made straight on himself. When she reached the cottage, she found a huntsman waiting to seize her, and turned away to the river. The Duke was close behind. The captive heard the distant shriek, — "Father, I come! I come!" — and saw her leap from the cliff into the stream. That night the father was less strictly watched, and escaped from his prison. He wandered along the banks of the river, till on a little beach of sand he saw, glimmering through the dark, a white heap, which was his daughter's body. He sat upon the sand till dawn, holding the corpse in his arms, and, when light began to break, carried it into the woods, and so, alternately resting and journeying all day, he at last reached his hut, dug a grave under the fallen leaves, and there buried his child. Thenceforth he never left the deep wood, nor heard tidings of man, till a horseman rode furiously through the thicket, and the horse stumbled and fell at the threshold of the hut. The rider was Duke Eberhard. He had been set upon when hunting in the forest by a band of his feudal enemies, and was desperately wounded. The recluse lifted him up, laid him on his own bed of leaves, and did what he could to revive him, so that, when he opened his eyes, the face that he saw bending over him was that of his former prisoner and vassal. Many were the strange and fearful words of rage and misery that the dying man uttered. He shrank and trembled, when his new attendant spoke to him; and he asked, "Wilt thou not murder me then?" It seemed from his language that the fair, pale image of Agnes had pursued him ever since her death, and frightened him forth often at midnight into the lonely forest. The phantom, he said, had driven him on to the spot where his enemies lay in wait for him; and when he was flying from them, and looked back to see if they were near, the only figure he discerned was that of the maiden running with her long hair fallen about her, as when in life she ran before him, and pointing a drawn sword at him. The childless father spoke to him of peace and pardon; but the Duke looked at him with fierce eyes, and groaning, "This from thee!" with one long breath expired. The peasant gave notice of the place and manner of Eberhard's death; and so his own abode became known to many. He began to be regarded as a holy hermit. The country people told, after his death, of miracles wrought beside his grave; and at last his name was canonized, and his bones were transferred to this great Abbey Church. But now for thee and me this time of preternatural awakening is wellnigh over. The life in each is but a weak spark of that which glowed in Eberhard and his vassal. In each of us doubtless it lingers for some reasonable purpose, whether one day to be re-united to its ampler source, or to take new shapes, and work for other than human ends in some different region of existence. Of this much be thou sure, that life is more and worthier than its outward agitations and clamours, — the sea larger and more stable than its bubbles There are millions of connected, concentric realities, ever revolving and unfolding themselves, which must each do its own work steadily, not dashing and exploding into the track of its neighbour. All these may, by the nobler intelligences, be studied and understood, if love, and faith, and patience be not wanting. But it is the prerogative of folly to fancy that revolt, display, noise, subjugation can be profitable for anything, and that, when these are impossible, existence stagnates. Writhing is not the truest grace, nor roaring the sweetest music of nature. The mad lightning-flash may deem that, as it bursts and passes, the stars too vanish with it. But they survive unchanged, and smile out calmly, when the storm has raged itself away.

Armour. Would that the dust of Eberhard could awaken, and with one blast of his horn dash to pieces these gloomy vaults, and for ever silence thy foolish prate beneath the ruins!

Skeleton. Even thy ravings are doubtless explicable, from the idea of a higher order than mortals can measure, which includes and justifies all things. But it is plain that thou hast not yet learnt thy destination, or that of the world; and much wilt thou have to endure in attaining to that knowledge.

The Caterpillar

An Unpublished Episode From The Royal Histories Of Abu Taleb

(From The Athenaeum, 1828)

The Caliph's tree, in the Royal Gardens at Bagdad, is it not as celebrated as the well Zemzem, the waters of which give beauty to women, and eloquence to the lips of the poet? Every one who has heard of Bagdad, knows that the stem is of pure gold, with branches of silver, and that each leaf is a separate jewel. The music which gushes amid its boughs by night and day, has reached to the corners of the earth; and its shadow is more delightful than the greenest bower in the four gardens of Asia. The Peris have often been seen to light upon it at sunset; and the gleam of their flower-like wings has mingled with the waving splendour of the tree, while the plaintive murmur of their voices sounded amid the breezy chimes of the rich and star-studded foliage, and the pipings of the opal-coloured or purple birds which nestled or fluttered in the leaves.

In the fifth year of the Caliph Mohadi, after the second hour of prayer, Zobeide, the most beautiful among the daughters of the Commander of the Faithful, was seated beneath its rainbow-tinted shade. This was but her fourteenth summer; yet a thousand poets had proclaimed her the noblest pearl in the diadem of Islam, and the brightest lamp of Paradise. While the light breezes floated past her, and flung their tributes of spicy scent among the long ringlets on her bosom, she sat upon a silken cushion, and twisted flowers into a garland for the neck of her favourite antelope.

But suddenly a large green and crimson caterpillar crept from a rosebud to the hand that held it. Zobeide started at feeling it on her finger, and flung it off hastily at the foot of the golden tree, where it lay for an instant bruised and motionless. A moment after, it swelled and rose, till it had expanded into the form of a venerable man, clothed in white robes, and leaning on a long ebony staff. He fixed his eyes upon Zobeide, and said, I am Buzurg Mihir, who alone of men was a true believer before the coming of the Prophet. Thou hast been permitted to read the sublime volume: wherefore hast thou not better learned its precepts, than to dash from thy hands an unoffending insect? God has given thee power to injure his creatures; but by the mouth of the Prophet he has commanded thee to protect them. Thou shalt speedily know thy punishment. At these words he frowned so fiercely, that Zobeide shuddered, and dropped her white eyelids with their dark fringes over her glancing eyes.

When she looked up, he was gone; but at the same time she saw a dark cloud advancing over the garden. An army of locusts was approaching, which filled the air around her, and hid the light with their innumerable legions. The ground under her feet became animated with frogs and lizards; and shining serpents crawled and hissed among the flowers of the garden. In an agony of alarm Zobeide shrieked and ran to the entrance; but, instead of the tall black slave who usually guarded it with his scymetar, an immense crocodile opened his long jaws, armed with tremendous teeth to oppose her passage, and beat the earth with his rattling tail, while the Princess felt as if every stroke was to crush her.

She rushed to another gate, and was stopped by an enormous web of thick black rope, which a spider, of the size of a camel, was engaged in completing. When she approached the creature, — for despair had made her courageous, — he desisted from his labour, stretched out six long arms, which terminated in crooked claws, grinned horribly in her face, and seemed prepared to drag her into the meshes of his den. She fled from this second opponent; but wherever she turned, some huge monster encountered her. The locusts filled and darkened the air; their noise perpetually sounded in her ears; and they had settled on every leaf in the garden. She tried every path to find some means of escape, but failed in them all; and at the last entrance a gigantic centipede reared himself on his tail, and with his horrid head overtopped the tallest palm-trees round him.

She started from the new enemy, and fell in a swoon upon the sod. When she recovered, Buzurg Mihir was before her. Zobeide, he said, thou art punished sufficiently. Remember in future to pity the meanest of the creatures of God.

The white robe fell from his figure; he dropped the staff; and the ancient sage was suddenly transformed into the noblest youth among the sons of Islam. The princess was enchanted by his green turban and purple slippers, his black mustachios, and sparkling eyes lighted with admiration; and the grace with which he hung around her neck a string of the largest pearls of Bahrein, made Hatem completely triumphant. In three days Zobeide was on her way to Syria with the Emir of Damascus, whom Arabia and Persia had unanimously declared to be brave as Rustam, generous as Arabah, and handsomer than Ferhad, the lover of Shirin. Zobeide never again hurt a caterpillar; for, fondly as she loved Hatem, she always abhorred the recollection of Buzurg Mihir.

Moral.

So far the veracious Abu Taleb; and hence young ladies may learn that the way to obtain handsome husbands is to kill caterpillars.

The Last of the Giants

(From The Athenaeum, 1828)

About the middle of the fifteenth century of our era, a brigantine, which had sailed from the Tagus, was wrecked on that north-western corner of the great continent of Africa, where the ancients placed Mount Atlas. The whole crew were lost on that inhospitable beach, with the exception of a single person. Roderick was a strong and daring man, of middle age, who in his wandering life had seen many changes. He had fought and acquired distinction in Italy, and had studied in Spain with such success, as to become master of several of the most ancient languages of the East, besides the fashionable sciences of logic, metaphysics, astronomy, medicine, and theology. His character was a singular mixture of the soldier and the philosopher. Amid the destruction of his comrades, he saved little more than his life, his sword, and a bag of hard biscuit, which had suffered considerably from the salt-water. Supported however by this bitter and scanty fare, he journeyed for some days towards the interior of the country. He travelled at night, to avoid the heat of the sun, and sought for rest and concealment by day; and he was compelled to eke out his sustenance by wild fruits. In this manner he made good his progress for thirty days; at the end of which time he found himself at the foot of a steeper, more rugged, and loftier mountain than any he had previously passed over. The full moon enabled him to examine the barrier which opposed him; and after some scrutiny he discovered a ravine, which led up the side of the vast eminence, and appeared to be the bed of a winter torrent. It was now dry; and he determined to pursue the course it marked out for him. After struggling upwards the whole night among rocks and sand, he found himself at daybreak still far from the summit; and discovering a small clump of trees, which shaded the side of the gorge, at no great distance, he resolved to repose there for the day. Some drops of water fortunately trickled through the rocks, among their roots; and when he had availed himself of this resource to quench his thirst, he stretched himself in the cool and dim retreat, and speedily sank to sleep. His slumber lasted for the greater part of the day. When he awoke, the sun had so far declined, that its disk seemed resting on the summit of the pass. He left the shade of the trees, beneath which he had spent the day, and gained the middle of the ravine. A considerable ledge of stone rose in his front, over which he climbed; and just when he had lifted his head above its edge, a noise like a sudden peal of thunder seemed to break from the height above. He raised his eyes in that direction, and saw rushing towards him a huge mass of rock, broken from the mountain, and rolling down with the speed of a torrent. It came on crushing the few trees that grew in its path, and shattering the crags on which it struck. Roderick crouched below the ledge he had been mounting; and the enormous block bounded over his head, and crashed downwards towards the plain. He immediately regained his former position; and his first impulse was to look up, for the purpose of discovering the cause which had loosened the crag, and placed him in so tremendous a peril. His eyes were directed to the break of the mountain, towards which he had been toiling; and he saw, standing against the sky, and showing dark between him and the sun, a being of such monstrous size, as no pageant had ever exhibited, no tale ever told of. The rocky soil was still crumbling under his foot; and some detached fragments, though smaller than the former, were bursting at intervals down the ravine. He leaned upon a cedar, which seemed recently up-rooted; and the hands clasped upon its top looked each of them larger than the largest shield employed in the wars of Europe. His head was bent down towards the plain; and, amid its grim and shaggy swarthiness, Roderick thought he could perceive a look of melancholy. Except that a diadem of gold encircled his grey hairs, his body was entirely destitute of ornament; and a girdle of lion-skins covering his loins was his only vesture. He stood thus mournfully surveying the wilderness for many minutes, and seemed a mighty colossus of granite fixed for ever upon the mountain. His shadow darkened the pass; and Roderick could perceive that it stretched for leagues over the desert. At last he turned himself slowly; and the light streamed in upon the darkness which he had made. He stretched his arm; and again the soldier felt the cold shadow on his brow. The object of his consternation gained with a few strides the very crest of the eminence, through a hollow of which the traveller had been labouring. The Giant sat down upon the summit, seemingly without perceiving that he had crushed a thicket beneath him. He leaned his head upon his arm, and let the cedar fall from his hand, as if it had been a wand. It dropped not far from Roderick; and he thought that no trunk of such prodigious measure had ever been nourished in the forests of Spain or

Germany. But he withdrew his eyes to look at the monster, and saw that he seemed to have composed himself to meditation. His limbs lay along the ridge of the mountain; he appeared to take in at a gaze the whole continent beneath him; and the outline of the giant, touched by the last splendour of the setting sun, showed in all the immensity of its proportions, with a distinctness which would have been beautiful, had it not been terrible.

But darkness came; and the being on whom Roderick looked, was no longer anything more than a shadow among shades, a mass, like a thunder-cloud, of threatening obscurity. The traveller remained motionless and silent. At last the giant lifted himself against the firmament, and disappeared behind the ridge of the mountain. Roderick pursued his way in much of fear, and something of perplexity; though he was less astonished at what he had seen, than the modern philosophers would have been, whom presumption has made sceptical. He proceeded up the pass, and after the labour of several hours approached its highest elevation. But long before he reached the top, he heard with surprise and alarm a succession of crashing noises, like the sound of a vessel's masts and timbers breaking in the tempest.

He arrived at the highest part of the gulley; and the mountains, on one of which he had before seen the Giant recline, rose high on each hand. The stars were out above the crags; and a bright moon clearly showed the whole wonderful prospect which lay before him. He had now gained access to a large and wooded valley, a basin among the hills, a part of which was occupied by a lake entering it at one side, and stretching away beyond his view. Into this receptacle ran a broad stream, which flowed from some unseen recess, and, directly beneath the position of the wanderer, fell in a considerable cataract, to gain the level of the lake. Fronting him at a distance, half-way up the opposite ascent, a red and smoky fire was blazing under the shadow of a cavern; and when he looked still higher towards the summit of the eminence, the great and fearful being he had already seen was moving with part of his figure clearly defined against the deep blue sky, as enormous as the phantom-seeming clouds of the crater of a volcano, but distinct as a statue of iron. Not statue-like however did he now stand; for he was engaged in a labour worthy even of his strength. On the very crest of the mountain a pile of wood was reared, larger than the largest of the Egyptian Pyramids; and to this the Giant was adding new loads of timber. He stepped with a few strides to the neighbouring hills, and encircling in his arms at once a score of the tallest trees, evidently the produce of many centuries, plucked them from the earth by the roots. The sound of their overthrow was that which had scared Roderick. The Titan snapped off their heads with all the foliage, as a child would break a lily, and returned deliberately with the trunks, to place them upon the already immeasurable heap. Thus he did repeatedly, till he had accumulated, from many leagues of forest, a structure of such magnitude, that it might have furnished materials for all the navies in the world, and would have out-topped the tower of Babylon, and covered a wider space than the palace of Nero. Roderick gazed upon the Giant and his labour with breathless awe. As he moved round the pile, his portentous frame was perpetually displayed in some new attitude, that called forth new astonishment, by exhibiting afresh the miracles of his size and power. Sometimes, when the pile appeared to incline too much on one side or the other, he applied both his hands to push it in the required direction; and, the moon pouring its full stream of light on his broad expanse of back, it seemed a steep ascent, rough with hair, and broken into a thousand varieties of surface by ridges of sinews and crags of bone, but wide enough for the charge of a hundred chariots; and the legs, which were then extended and active, showed like leaning towers with pillar-work of muscles. Or, in adding to the height of the fabric, he would lift his arm to its full length between the view of Roderick and the sky, holding some immense trunk with its recent roots gleaming white in the moonshine. On such occasions it seemed that he could have swept the stars from their courses, and dashed away the empyrean, as a robber tears off the veil of his captive. The golden circlet which he still wore, glittered on his forehead far up amid the sky, like one of the heavenly orbs; and he looked as if he had indeed a right to add his diadem to the number of the planets, and reign himself the Lord of the Universe.

The stranger had no conception for what purpose such a being could have erected such a pile. But for the time his attention was called away. The Giant descended the mountain, till he reached the cave in which the fire was still burning. He stooped to enter its recesses, though a galley in full sail might have passed beneath the arch without vailing its pennon, and returned, bearing in his right-hand a golden cup, of the size and shape of one of the domes of St. Sophia, and in his left a blazing tree. Carrying these, he bestrode the valleys as a ploughman steps across the furrows, till he arrived at the river. He dipped his bowl into the flood above the cataract; and for a moment the water-course was dry, and the noise of the falling torrent hushed. He stood up; he looked around him, and drank. Again the water had begun to flow, and the cataract roared between his feet; again he stooped; and again he had scooped the whole current into his vase; and the sound of the stream dashing over the rocks was not heard for some seconds. This time he did not empty the cup; but he bore it and the still burning trunk to his pile upon the mountain. He stood beside it, and flung over it some of the water; and, while he lifted the flaming brand, he looked towards the stars, and spoke aloud. Roderick started, when he heard his voice, not merely on account of the thrilling depth of tone, but because the language was one of those ancient tongues, with which the traveller had become familiar in his youth, having learned them from an aged Moor accomplished in all the knowledge of the East. As nearly as he could discover, the purport of that which the Giant uttered was as follows.

To you, O stars, with whom, and with whose inhabitants, I claim a kindred that belongs not to the insect-men of this lower earth, — to you I address myself; and in your honour I pour this water over the pile, whereon I am about to die. The child of a mighty line, the one surviver of a myriad kings, looks for the last time on your bright fronts, ye eternal orbs, and tells you that the sole remaining monarch of all the race, your offspring and your worshipers, is soon to seek the throne which awaits him amid your constellations. I have seen the sons of the giants fade away, as the forest which even now has fallen beneath my hand; and the world is given to a meaner kind, as that forest will be succeeded by a crop of weeds. Before this globe was divided into land and sea, before the parents of its present puny tribes had been formed out of its dust, it was the inheritance and the kingdom of my fathers. Ours were the structures, among the foundations of which men wander, and marvel at their height; ours the castle which scaled the skies; ours the mountains heaped on mountains, whereby we threatened to interrupt the revolutions of the sun. My sires wooed the spirits from other spheres, to become their brides and the mothers of their children; and the fire of angelic natures is in my veins. But that fire is now cold and dim; and I go to find, at your unfailing altars, the flame which may reanimate my soul. For five thousand years I have been alone on earth; and from the day when my hands reared Caucasus with all its peaks over the ashes of my father, I have seen none whose presence has not been a curse to me, — to whom I have not been a curse and a perdition. I have lived to keep burning among these mountains the holy flame which is grateful to you. But the destiny which has been over all my brethren, is over me; and my hour is come. The brightness of your power has been upon me in the nights of many ages. I can no longer resist the doom. I go to join you; I yield up this weary body to the elements from which it was composed. But while my dust shall be added to the clay of this globe, which is no longer the heritage of more powerful beings than man, — while the atoms of my body are resolved into that which may one day be trampled by the feet, and divided by the ploughshares, of the most wretched among mortals, — there is that within the fleshly frame, which shall become a sharer in your glory, and a portion of it. Look, you eternal orbs! and thou, moon! that even now art sinking from the heavens, look with your most splendid and benignant radiance on the death-fire of the Last of the Giants!

He applied his torch to the corners of the pile, and stood beside it with motionless serenity, looking steadfastly at the heavens, till the lapse of a considerable time had enabled the flames to deepen and to spread. They extended swiftly, with a thick smoke and a tremendous noise, till they had embraced the whole circuit of the pile, which then had more resemblance to a stormy and lurid sunset, than to any other spectacle known among men. The fire rushed furiously upward, and illuminated the form and face of the Titan with a light more unearthly and terrific than any in which the wanderer had seen him; and his broad eye fixed upon the moon gleamed like the corslet of a warrior on the wall of a burning city. But he did not long remain thus; for so soon as the whole mass of timber appeared to have caught the flame, he calmly stepped into the midst of the conflagration, and laid himself upon his scorching bed. The fire rose rapidly and far, till it widened and towered into a pyramid of light; and the grey smoke which burst around, darkened half the heavens. The wind increased; and the crackling of the wood, and roar of the burning became appalling. Clouds began to sail in over the opposite mountains; and, but for the glare of the pyre, the whole horizon would have been black. The blaze spread to the relics of the forest, and caught the brushwood which still covered a large portion of the hills. The prospect became one vast amphitheatre of fire; and the smoke and flame broke fiercely upward, and formed a sky of mingled light and darkness, sublimity and horror. Still the great master conflagration rose far beyond every other part of the burning circle, and seemed a furnace fuelled with the earth to consume the heavens. The eagles rose screaming from their nests upon the rocky peaks, and wheeled amid the smoke and flakes of fire, till even their wings were insufficient to bear them from the danger; and they dropped stifled into the red abyss. Roderick was compelled by the heat and smoke to flee from the danger. For several hours he travelled with the utmost speed away from the spot of so astounding a catastrophe, and at last lay down completely exhausted in a grotto among the rocks at the foot of the mountain. At the end of three days the clouds which had been gathering in the heavens, poured out their burthens. For a week the rain fell in a continued flood; and if the traveller had not been possessed of a small store of berries and nuts, he must have died of starvation. After that time the deluge ceased; and he returned upon his former steps to examine the Giant's valley; but the torrents had so roughened the ravine, that his journey was one of difficulty and pain. At length however he gained his goal, and found that the space encircled by the mountains was half filled with water, which had risen above the mouth of the cave. In this Roderick had expected to find some tokens and memorials of the Giant's existence; but it was now accessible only to the fishes and the water-snakes. He climbed to the bare summit of the mountain on which the pile had been raised, and found that the floods had washed away every vestige of the sacrifice he had witnessed. But on scrutinizing the surrounding rocks, which were all discoloured by the heat, he found in a crevice the well-remembered golden crown. It was adorned with graven devices of stars and wings, and framed of the purest metal. After months of toil and hardship, Roderick escaped to Europe; and a fragment of the diadem, which was all he had been enabled to save, sufficed in his native country to purchase broad lands, stately castles, and ancient lordships. But what was the grandeur of ordinary men to eyes that had beheld the mighty presence of the Last of the Giants?

The Shell

A Historical Apologue

(From The Athenaeum, 1828)

The world was made for man, said he.

I will tell you an apologue, answered the teacher.

1. In a beautiful bay of the celebrated island Atlantis, a large Shell of the most delicate white and the most rounded form, the relic from some previous world, lay on the smooth and elastic sand. It was left for a long period undisturbed and unaltered, sometimes kissed by the extreme bubbles of the billows, and often trembling so melodiously in the wind, as to have furnished to the early gods the first hint of a musical instrument, and to have been the prototype of the sounding conchs which accompanied with their deep notes the feasts on Olympus, and the Indian triumphs of Bacchus.

2. The moist dust gradually accumulated within it; and the germ of a sea-weed fell upon the soil, and grew until a fair and flourishing plant, with long dark leaves, overhung the white edge of the thin and moonlike vase. For many months the ocean-herb retained its quiet existence, imbibed the night-dew of the heavens, rejoiced in the fresh breezes from the sea, and lived in tranquil safety through every change of shower and sunshine. At length a storm arose, which rolled the waters upon the shore. The Shell was overwhelmed, the plant washed out of it, and the light

vessel swept into a cleft of the rocks.

3. After some days of calm and warmth, a bird dropped a seed into it, which sprouted and became an orange-tree. Its leaves were so thick and green, that they would have supplied a graceful chaplet to a wood-nymph; and she might have delighted to place in her bosom the pearly and fragrant blossoms which hung amid the tuft of verdure. The seasons with their varieties, and the starry influences of gentle nights nurtured the shrub; and the pure flowers were changed into gorgeous fruits, which gleamed through the foliage like the glimpses of a gilded statue in some deserted temple through the robes and coronals of creepers which have overgrown it. The orange-tree had gladdened many springtimes with its sweetness and its splendour, when it faded and died; and the birds of the air piped a lamentation over the shrub, amid the living beauty of which they had so often nestled.

4. In after years, when nothing remained of the orange but a slight and dreamy odour around the Shell, and the last light grains of the dust wherein it grew had been borne away by the eddying breezes, a butterfly, as red and glittering as the planet Mars, came on its crimson wings to the dim and spiral cell. It fluttered round the ivory entrance, poised itself upon it for a moment, and waved its silken sails. Then, after darting and circling, like a winged mote of the sunbeam, through the deep woods and over the sea, it returned to perish. While it sank into its quiet and beautiful retreat, it yet seemed loth to leave a world which to it had been a fairy domain: but the necessity of its nature was upon it; and it closed the gay leaflets which had sustained its flight, and resigned itself to death.

5. It was followed by a troop of bees, which took possession of the Shell, and, after their daily excursions over meadow and bloomy bank, returned to its smooth and undulated chambers with the materials of their combs, and with large store of bright and luscious honey. The tiny echoes of their abode resounded with the constant hum of labour and happiness; and it was soon as brimming as a wine-cup at a nuptial-feast, with the rich and perfumed treasures of the insects, arranged and sealed in the exact compartments which filled the interior of their silvery palace. But a bird attacked and destroyed their commonwealth; and again the Shell was left empty.

6. A humming-bird, all emerald, ruby, and sapphire, then discovered the lonely nook, and folded its jewelled wings there. It soon found a mate; and together they lived a flowery life. He who had seen either of them wandering at sunset through the glen, would have believed that the brilliant core of the western sky was fluttering away along the earth; or the little animal might have been thought the choicest signet of a prince, transformed of a sudden into a living thing, and endued with the power of flight. When they wheeled together towards their home at twilight, no pair of fire-flies, no twin lights of the firmament could be brighter than their diamond crests. The sweet essences of a thousand buds and flowers supplied their nourishment; and, while they sucked the delicious juices of ripe fruits, their wings were tinctured by the lightest bloom of the plum and the grape. But the rain dropped thick and fast into the Shell; and the gentle birds, which seemed made to whisper love-messages in the rosebud ear of a lady, and to hide themselves in sport among her ringlets, departed from their

nest, and sought, in sparry grotto, or in southern bower, a more secure habitation for their lovely, but frail existence.

7. Lastly, at sun-rise, seemed flitting from the morning-star an elfin spirit, which danced into the Shell, and assumed it as his home. It thrilled with life and pulsation; and while a spring gushed out of the rock, and bore it along towards the sea, he spread his thin wings to the breeze, and sailed in his lily-coloured argosy away over the blue and sunny deep. The white Shell, and its new sovereign, moved forward with the graceful swiftness of a snowy swan, tilting over the light ripples of the water, and, when night came with its constellations, seemed to be itself a trembling star on the verge of the horizon. That spirit too shall inhabit the Shell but for a time, and shall then depart, that he may develop, in some more fitting position, the whole capacities of his nature. The Shell will sink into the waves, and be joined to the treasures of the ocean caverns, in them also to aid the existence of other beings, and to fulfil a new cycle of its ministry.

That Shell is the WORLD; that Spirit MAN. Yet not for man alone was it created, but for all the living things in the successive stages of existence, which can find in it a means of happiness, and an instrument of the laws which govern their being.

Zamor

(From The Athenaeum, 1828)

I

The air was basking in the noontide among the hills that are traversed by the rapid Erigon. The woody sides of the valleys which opened upon the river, lay slumbering in breezy dimness; but the sky was blue and bright around the breasts and peaks of the mountains, except where broad white clouds, floating high and swift between them and the sun, varied the landscape by occasional sweeps of shadow. The sparkling and winding water flowed silently along the green bases of the eminences; and its surface was marked by nothing but the differences of colour occasioned by the wind and stream, and by the fresh-looking islets of water-plants, or the trunk of a tree rolling down the current, and showing its brown branches or the white rent of its stem among the shining ripples. Down one of the glens which descend towards the stream, a boy of thirteen or fourteen years of age was slowly wandering. He was tall and of a noble presence. His open, upturned brow was surrounded with careless ringlets of light brown hair, and was shaded by a low cap or bonnet, in which he wore an eagle's feather. His dark-coloured kirtle descended to his knee, over trowsers which left the leg exposed above the sandal. A belt of wolf-skin sustained a short sword, and confined his dress round the waist; and with his left hand he led a large and powerful dog by a twisted chain of gold; while in his right he carried a strong hunting spear, the point of which gleamed like a star above his head. His features were of a regular and spirited beauty; and his quick eye perpetually glanced from the path he was pursuing to the mountains round him and the skies beyond. He proceeded in his devious and negligent course, now sinking into thought, now rushing and leaping over rocks and bushes, while the dog sprang up and barked and sported round him, till he reached an irregular and broken wood, which spread, with many intervals, along the green banks of the river.

The boy threw himself under the shade of an oak, where he had a glimpse of the cool water among the stems of the trees; and his canine friend couched quietly by his side, now looking up into his face, now rubbing his legs with its nose, and wagging its bushy tail, now closing its eyes, and sinking with a sigh into a tranquil doze. The youth too was so still, that he might have been thought to slumber, had not his restless glances indicated the stir within. It was indeed a mind not formed for inactivity; but its present thoughts were rather the overflowing and sport of its vigour, than the application of it to any definite end. He remembered the oracles which had spoken among the ancient oaks of Epirus, till he almost heard the promise of his own greatness sounding from the trees, while they trembled and rustled around and above him. Then came imaginations of the Dryads, the forest spirits, so beautiful and so capricious, who were accustomed to fly from men, and dedicate their loveliness to the greenwood shade. As the breeze moved the shadow of some branch, he started to think that he saw the waving of the airy locks; and for a moment he beheld the twinkle of the light footsteps, in the casual breach of a sunbeam through the foliage on the dark ground of the vistas before him. These visions passed away; and in their place seemed sweeping through the distant obscurity of the thicket the pomp and triumph of Bacchus, — the youths with arms and wine-cups, and baskets of gorgeous fruits unknown to Europe, the dark eyes and glowing limbs of damsels, whose wreaths of Oriental flowers shook fragrance through the air, while swiftly and gracefully they flung aloft and struck together their ringing cymbals, ancient Pan with a world of merriment in his pipe, and, amid a tumult of green coronals and wild exultations, the young conqueror himself, drawn forward by his lions, with the pride of a hundred victories on his brow, and the joyousness of a hundred vintages on his lips, and a spear so often washed in wine, and so clustered with grapes and ivy-berries, half-hid among their foliage, that not a trace of its myriad death-stains was visible. They gleamed for a moment from the recesses of the green maze on the eye of the dreaming boy; and why should not he too be the conqueror of Asia, and his banners return over the Hellespont laden and glittering with the spoils of the Euphrates and the Indus?

He rose while he thought of it, so hastily that his dog gave a slight cry at feeling the pull which his collar received from the arm of his master, who stept forward eagerly for an instant, while his right hand grasped the spear with an energy indicating how bold would be the spirit and how wide the fame of Alexander, the son of Philip.

He walked forward for a few minutes with boyish impetuosity, when his attention was diverted by seeing a large blue butterfly, which flew across his path. He freed the chain which held Lacon from the collar, and pursued the insect; while the dog, in imitation of his master, rushed barking and eager in pursuit of the same wandering object. It led him among the hills which he had before left, never coming within his reach, but never mounting so far away as to make him relinquish the pursuit. It flew at last over the edge of a precipice into a broken and narrow dell; but the fearless and active boy dropped from the verge, and, after scrambling for a minute or two among the rocks and bushes, reached the end of the descent. It was a wild and lonely hollow, on the steep banks and narrow area of which the pine and the cypress rose above the thick under-growth of weeds, shrubs, and flowers. The insect still hovered before its pursuer; and, after a few steps, he found that he had followed it into an ancient cemetery. The tombs seemed to have been mouldering in neglect for centuries; and merely a few irregular mounds and broken fragments of walls remained. Beyond one of these relics of building, now covered with different vigorous creepers, the bright blue wings disappeared. He went to the spot, and found that, beyond the dilapidated wall, the sun streamed in upon a little patch of grass. Here the insect had poised itself upon a human skull, half covered with moss, and crowned by a natural wreath of trailing honey-suckle. Thus the beautiful and airy creature he had been chasing was perched, with its azure fans expanded and glittering in the sunshine. It seemed the immortal Psyche, the spiritual life waiting to take wing from amid the dust and decay of mortality. The boy leaped over the obstruction, and stooped to seize it; but it vibrated for an instant the splendid pennons which served it for sails, and rose swiftly and far above the head of the disappointed pursuer.

He looked after it for a few seconds; and Lacon bayed fiercely at the soaring insect. But his owner stooped again to the relic; for, when he had previously bent towards the butterfly, he had seen what appeared to be metal shining on the turf. It was a large gold coin, which lay between the teeth of the skull. The device of an eye within a circle was distinctly visible on one side; and on the other was traced, in the oldest character Alexander had ever seen, the word ZAMOR.

He restored the coin to its place; but such was his recollection of the occurrence, that the signet, wherewith in after years he sealed Hephæstion's lips, bore the device of a butterfly poised upon a skull, with the motto ZAMOR.

‖

The youth was a youth no more. He was in all the vigour and beauty of manhood, a sovereign and a conqueror, and roamed no longer in the woods of Macedonia, but in the deep gloom of an Indian forest. He had outstripped his train in the eagerness of the chase; and when the thick jungle prevented him from continuing his course on horseback, he leaped from the saddle and pierced his way on foot. His mantle was now of regal splendour; and his light helmet was encircled with a slender diadem of gold. The garment which fell from under his inlaid cuirass to his knee, was interwoven with silver thread; and his sandals were studded with jewels. His lips had gained the firm expression of will and power; and thought had left its stamp upon his forehead.

He penetrated speedily through the thicket which had interrupted him, and found himself in a little glade surrounded by spreading trees. He stood still, and gazed for a moment; and it seemed to him that he heard the half-stifled sobs of sorrow not far off. He moved in the direction of the sound, and, after pushing through a screen of bushes, found himself near an old man, who was kneeling on the ground, close to the trunk of a great tree; and, while his clasped hands trembled on his shuddering breast, the tears fell thickly from his eyes. He wore the dress of a Brahmin. Beside him lay the corpse of a girl, apparently twelve or thirteen years of age. Though her skin was rather more dusky than that of Europeans, she was very beautiful in the eyes of the king. Her round and shining limbs were of the most exquisite delicacy; the long black hair, wreathed with white flowers, fell loose over her maiden bosom, which had ceased to heave with the breath of life. An arrow had pierced her through the body; and the blood had flowed to the knees of the old man, and stained his garments. He was a father wailing over his murdered child.

Alexander silently approached, and saw that on the left breast of the lovely form, in which the heart no longer stirred, a blue butterfly had placed itself. The agony and tears of the parent did not disturb it. He touched the hair and fingers of the body with a trembling affection, and gazed at it long and passionately; and then again his whole frame was shaken; and he burst into a paroxysm of grief. As the king drew near, the insect rose and soared away to the heavens. Alas! that like it the corpse could not raise itself from the dust it adorned, and move again in all the vivacity and grace of its former existence!

The conqueror spoke in a low, reverential, and sympathizing voice to the bereaved father. The old man started at the sound, rose to his feet, and shook off the tokens of his agony, as far as nature permitted him. Alexander asked him by what misfortune he had lost his daughter. The soldiers, replied the Brahmin, of the insane and cruel invader, who has attacked our country, seized my child, and would have detained her, but that she escaped by flight from their hands, when one of them shot an arrow, which slew my beautiful and my beloved.

I swear by the gods, they shall be punished; but do you know, old man, to whom you speak, that you thus venture to calumniate the great Alexander?

If I could not judge by the vulgar signs of those gay and fantastic trappings, I should yet recognize the eyes which so readily glare, the nostril that dilates, the brow that contracts, with passion. These all mark the man who has been accustomed to command others, but not himself.

This is a sight, replied the king, pointing to the dead body, which prompts me to forgive your boldness.

It is a sight, O king, which should rather teach you that I do not need your forgiveness. You have robbed my earthly existence of its charm and glory. I care not how soon it may end.

This is philosophy which would have pleased Callisthenes. What is your name and condition?

I am called Sabas; and, after having travelled over many countries, and learned your language in the Lesser Asia, I have lived, and been happy, — here he faltered, and looked at his child, — at the tomb of the sage ZAMOR.

The warrior started at the name, and asked of Sabas, who was ZAMOR. The Brahmin replied that he had lived many ages before, and had been a mighty conqueror; but that, after overrunning half the earth, he had flung away at once the sceptre and the sword, and betaken himself to a life of meditation and benevolence. The old man went on to say, that the king would learn more from the chief of the Brahmins, who attended the tomb; and to him Sabas brought Alexander.

The ancient teacher, to whom the Grecian commander was thus introduced, trembled in his presence, and, on his demanding to know something more about ZAMOR, replied, that, in addition to what Sabas had told him, the following information was all he could supply: the venerated being in question had employed the later moments of his protracted life in giving directions as to the place and manner in which his ashes were to be disposed of; and, in the volume of pure morality and sublime devotion which he had left, it was declared that the iron doors which bounded his sepulchre would never open, till one who had been as great a conqueror should demand admission. In the course of many ages none such had presented himself.

The pride and curiosity of the sovereign were aroused; and he desired to be led to the tomb. The Brahmin summoned his brethren; and in long files they preceded Alexander to the cavern.

Its rocky circuit was of sufficient extent to include them all: they ranged themselves around the sides; and their leader and the monarch advanced to the tomb, on which several lamps were burning. Here the chief Brahmin offered up his prayers, while the Macedonian went forward to the doors at the farther extremity, and, to the horror of the throng, violently smote the massy metal with the hilt of his sword. The doors crashed open slowly, and displayed a staircase. The king descended fearlessly and alone; and after a long absence returned with a haggard countenance and disordered steps to the cavern, while the doors closed suddenly behind him. He seemed at first confused and bewildered; but, soon recovering himself, he looked round him at the Brahmins, and said, I know not whether you have a share in yonder mummery; but at all events let a wall be built across that entrance, sufficient to prevent any future attempts like mine.

He had paused, and seemed relapsing into deep and doubtful thought, when a loud rush and clang was heard without, mingled with the sound of trumpets. Alexander knew the notes, and, resuming the soldier and the king, gravely saluted the generals, who had sprung from their horses, and entered the cave to seek him. He moved before them to the mouth of the cavern, and found his usual train of several hundred horsemen, with the chief nobility of Macedonia, Greece, and Persia, awaiting his appearance. Innumerable varieties of dress and arms, of language and feature, were here assembled; and every province he ruled over had sent its noblest and most splendid inhabitants to swell the court of Alexander. All were mounted on the fleetest and most beautiful coursers of Thessaly and Asia; and an unrivalled steed was led by the grooms of the monarch. He mounted it with a careless bound; and while he galloped from the spot, followed by the glittering whirlwind of officers, feudatories, and kings, he talked to those around him of the battle, the chase, the banquet, the philosophy of Aristotle, and the charms of Paneaste.

III

The day had died in storm; and the chamber of Alexander was closed and lighted. He lay on his couch in the restlessness and pain of a fever, from which he was never to recover.

He was attended only by a young Persian girl, who watched his lightest word and sign with far more than the carefulness of servility. There was all the intensity of passionate affection in that pale cheek, those tearful eyes, and that quivering forehead. She moved silently through the splendid room at the least hint of the patient's want; and, when it was satisfied, she would sit down and weep in silence.

It was early in the evening when he said, Abra, I would speak with Perdiccas. She flew from the chamber, and in a few moments returned with the person named, and then retired to the antechamber; where, among slaves, guards, attendants, and physicians, she hid her face in her hands, and sobbed bitterly, while she thought that the man she loved would so soon breathe his last.

Perdiccas entered the room silently and slowly, and sat beside the bed. After a few moments of heavy breathing, the King turned towards his friend, and told him to move the lamp, so that it might throw no light on the couch. He then proceeded thus:

Perdiccas, you will remember having once found me in India, at the tomb of ZAMOR. I have revealed to no man what I saw there; but I will now disclose it to you. The circumstances which led me thither are of little importance. Suffice it that I presented myself at the iron gates, and that they opened to admit me. I proceeded down a long and dark flight of steps, then through a passage, then down other steps, and had at last advanced to an immense distance through the rock. I thought for a moment of returning; but I went on, and travelled, as it seemed, league after league. At length I reached an iron grating, which with some difficulty I pushed open, and found myself in a large chamber. On the opposite wall there appeared to be a faint glimmer of light; and to it I proceeded. I touched the spot; and it felt like the side of a tent: I found that it was a curtain covering an aperture; I pulled it aside; and a broad pale light burst upon me through the opening, which also gave me a view of another, and far larger chamber than that in which I stood.

The room into which I looked was a vast gallery, which stretched its dreary vista almost beyond the sight. The floor was of black marble, and the sides of polished porphyry. Along the walls thrones were ranged at equal spaces, to an interminable distance. Those on one side were all occupied, except the nearest, which bore the name of ZAMOR, but which his late penitence and imperfect reparation had saved the ancient conqueror from occupying. The throne opposite to this, — the first in the vacant line, — was inscribed, ALEXANDER. And O Perdiccas! could I speak with the tongue of one of those Athenian poets, whose renown will be as great as mine, I should yet be unable to express the tithe of that horror which seized me, when I looked upon the tenants of those other thrones, and saw that a similar one was destined for me. It is not that they had an aged or barbaric appearance, — though their hairs were white, and their brows haggard, and their dresses were those of the East and of the North: but their faces were marked with a still desperation, and their bodies settled in a calm agony, of which I had no previous conception. I have often looked upon death: but no pangs from the sword, or from the torture, ever seemed to me more than a slight discomfort, compared to the sufferings of those mighty and glorious warriors. They sat motionless as the rocks on the banks of Phlegethon; but it was the tranquillity of an endurance which feels that it would be hopeless to attempt escape. The eyes of some were nearly closed; and there seemed no light in their countenances, but a dull dead glare which escaped from beneath their shadowing eyelids. There was one hoary head and swarthy cheek, with a diadem of jewels, and the Egyptian beetle on his breast; and I knew the presence of Sesostris. And there was ancient Belus, with the star of the Babylonian wizards on his brow, leaning his awful head upon his hand. And there was the warrior-deity of those Scythians, whom in my boyhood I subdued, clothed in wolf-skins, but with a cuirass on his breast, and a crown of iron around his scarred forehead. Hercules too, whom we have dreamed a god, leaned upon his club in anguish, which, though silent, was more horrible than the pangs he endured from the robe of Nessus; and a greater than he, or than all the rest, showed the writhen features and sunken cheeks of long-sustained suffering, beneath those emblems of mysterious strength, the moonlike horns of Ammon.

There was one spirit, and but one, in whom the fiery energy of his nature was not repressed by the tremendous fate to which he was subjected, — the Greek, who in his youth was victor over Asia, the fleetest, the most beautiful, the bravest, the most unhappy, the demigod Achilles. His eyes still shone like stars, amid the burning halo wherewith his head was of old encircled by Minerva, and which still beamed around him, as if in mockery of those white lips compressed and agitated with a paroxysm of affliction too mighty even for the slayer of Hector to master it. In the shield which leant against his knees, I saw not the images of the harvest and the dance, but the reflection of the hero's immeasurable pain.

The feet of each of these terrible shadows were placed upon an image of the world; and before my throne I saw a similar attribute. My empire seemed to clasp with its boundary an enormous portion of the earth; but its limits were faint and wavering; and methought at every instant they shrank and broke asunder. Above the thrones were trophies; but, in the midst of each of them, that grey, stern Destiny, who, from its iron cave in some distant planet, sends forth the silent blasts that sway the universe, had fixed some emblem of mockery, shame, and evil. The mowing ape, the crawling worm, the foulness of the harpy, the envenomed slime of the serpent, showed themselves among the spoils, weapons, crowns, and banners of royalty and conquest. And over all this a ghastly light was shed from the eyeless sockets of skeleton warders, who waited upon the enthroned victims.

Can you wonder, my friend, that I felt a horror, which swords and flames and menacing millions could not inspire, when I gazed upon the eternal agonies of those beings so dead to all but misery? My eyes almost failed to see, and my feet to stand, when I turned from them to mark the throne, which bore, so deeply engraven on its granite pedestal, the name of Alexander. From that hour my nature has changed. I have not had the resolution to yield up my conquests, and disrobe myself of my greatness; but I have sought to lose the memory of my former deeds and future doom in revelries and intoxications, which at last have brought me death, though they have never bestowed forgetfulness. I shall soon be among those dreary and tormented shadows of departed power and dearly bought renown. Take you this ring, (and he gave him the emblematic signet,) and, when you look upon it, remember, that not the image you see upon it, of immortal life and unbroken happiness, will dwell with the remains of kings and conquerors, but the polluting earth-worm and the stinging scorpion.

His voice had grown hoarse and broken; and he proceeded slowly and feebly: though I have failed to profit by the lesson, thus much I have been taught by ZAMOR.

He never spoke again. He left for his generals the slavery of Greece and the distraction of the world; to Perdiccas, a counsel by which he had not profited himself; to Abra, a desolate existence and a broken heart. And so did he perish at Babylon, whose boyhood had sped so blithely among the hills of Macedonia.

Cydon

(From The Athenaeum, 1829)

The decay and corruption of Athens were more beautiful and impressive than ever was the decline of any other state. When, instead of severe religion and venerable laws, no power remained in the city of Pallas but the genius of Pericles, he concealed and brightened the ruins of ancient virtue with so much of intellectual excitement and refined pleasure, that men could scarcely fail to doubt whether the most solid and living substance of Good were worth the sparkling and intoxicating delusions which had been substituted for it.

At this time the abode of one extraordinary woman furnished a kind and a variety of enjoyments, to which the world had till then beheld nothing at all similar, and attracted a society in which the most celebrated and wonderful minds of Athens were proud to find a place. Aspasia, the mistress, the queen, the inspiring goddess of this spot, in which so many sources of amusement, so many persons of renown were brought together, was herself more fascinating and remarkable than aught or any one within the pale of delight that surrounded her. Her beauty was of the most voluptuous Ionian mould, illuminated and strengthened by an intellect such as had belonged to no woman before her, and has probably been given to very few in later times. The large dark eyes of her country were in her of the richest and deepest loveliness, and served moreover to aid the expression of an eloquence, from which Pericles, the glory of Athenian speakers, and Socrates, as drawn by Plato, borrowed the awful peals and subtle lightnings of their noblest discourses. Her form had the perfect symmetry required by sculptors, and so seldom discovered except in a few of their productions; and its movements satiated the eye and the fancy with the airy softness peculiar to the females of the Asiatic shore. But that form and inimitable grace appeared endowed with a new charm, when displayed in the mimic dances, which embodied the conceptions of poetry in images of a beauty far more exquisite, and far, alas! more fleeting, than that of the painter's creation. To all this must be added, that her knowledge of poetry and the arts put her on a level with the dramatists, the singers, the sculptors, and architects, who were themselves the delight of Greece, and who sought more eagerly for her approbation of their skill, than for that of their whole nation assembled at Elis or Corinth. Her manners moreover were marked with the most admirable ease, gentleness, and spirit; and she alone of those women, who have rashly wandered for applause beyond the circle of their homes, was able to conceal, if not subdue, the restless cravings of vanity, which are so much less satisfactory to others after the first moments of their surprise and excitement, than even the indifference of stagnant dulness.

The house in which she lived was one of the largest and handsomest at Athens, where the appearance of the private buildings was strongly contrasted with the ample magnificence of the public edifices. Aspasia, to whom, as a foreigner, the state was less a source of enjoyment and dignity, than to women connected with it by legal rights and sacred privileges, had felt the want of a domestic importance and splendour, that should in some sort afford her compensation. Pericles had gratified her taste and ambition; and his riches, and the admiration of the wealthiest and most powerful Athenians, and of the most accomplished artists in the world, had filled her abode with foreign rarities, with the most delicately shaped and painted vases, and with innumerable graceful devices in bronze and marble. Her apartments might thus have been thought a new Delphi, consecrated to Eros and the Graces, and as brilliantly ornamented with appropriate offerings and masterpieces, as was the Temple of Apollo with the trophies or spoils of victory, the offerings of cities, the statues of heroes and of gods.

Hither congregated the men, whose names have been through all succeeding time the watchwords of genius and glory. Anaxagoras, the philosopher, and Cratinus, the comic poet, in his extreme old age, brought their wisdom and their wit to the society of Aspasia. Sophocles delighted his beautiful hostess with a temper full of higher and more genial poetry, than all the eloquence in which Euripides exaggerated his sensibility, his passions, and his scepticism. The young Thucydides came to be instructed in civil knowledge by Pericles, to whom the younger Socrates in turn taught a deeper and more precious lore. When Gorgias attempted to declaim or to dispute, he was gravely conquered or laughably parodied by Aspasia. Panænus consoled himself in her company at his painting's having been excelled by Timagoras; and Phidias and Ictinus drew from her the inspiration and rules of those wonders of architecture and sculpture, which she had incited Pericles to command, and the execution of which was submitted to her judgement by the immortal artists. And Pericles himself, the general, the orator, the statesman, the hand, the tongue, the eye, and genius of Athens, while he displayed his love for her with a grave and devoted enthusiasm, maintained with playful dignity his immense superiority in will and in station over all who approached him.

Among the acquaintances of Aspasia, the women were not the least celebrated nor the least admired. Aspasia herself stood prominently forth, as of a different rank and fame from her whole sex. The constant and respectful attachment of Pericles would alone have been sufficient to procure her this estimation; but it was still more certainly secured by her own powers. Yet, though endowed with rarer beauty and faculties than all others, she was still the representative of a numerous class. The increase of luxury, the excessive refinement of taste and sensibility, the sharpened hunger for excitement of every kind, in a city where the intellect and the arts were so highly cultivated, the direction which this love of pleasure had taken towards the enjoyments of fancy and sympathy, — all this had created a demand for a species of social relaxation and of female intercourse, very different from what had been known in Greece in the days of its domestic simplicity. In the same way the love of the fine arts, of polished society, of fame, whose chosen haunt was the Acropolis and Agora of Athens, and of wealth, which commerce and political power had heaped in the same city, — this complicated feeling had drawn many a soft, impassioned, and accomplished Asiatic maid of Greek extraction to the spot which united more prizes for vanity, sensibility, and ambition, than all the world beside. Of such women, the most beautiful, the best instructed, the most attractive entreated permission to appear in the house of Aspasia. Nor was she to be very severely blamed for the character she played, and for the associates with whom it connected her. The force of her talents, the fiery eagerness of her longings for the gratification of the intellect, had brought her to the polite and brilliant capital of the Ionian tribes. Her habits, and her affection for Pericles detained her there; yet so long as she made it her residence her marriage was necessarily invalid, her children illegitimate, and she could hardly avoid the company of women, whose country, class, and position were in most respects the same as her own. Nothing therefore could be more splendid, nothing more animating, nothing more seductive, than the female band who shone and smiled, sang, danced, and acted, revelled and conversed in the apartments of Aspasia, and alternately amused and excited the wisest and most famous of their male contemporaries.

Such were the members of an assembly, which frequently met, and always with fresh desire to meet again, and with fresh admiration of Aspasia. On one of these occasions the conversation turned on sculpture; and Phidias took the opportunity of saying that he had lately obtained a new and distinguished pupil, a young Athenian, by name Cydon, who had spent several years at Sicyon in the school of Polycletus, and had now returned to his native city, and placed himself under the great rival sculptor. "His genius," added the master, "is of the highest order; and he alone has satisfied me in executing the works, with which thou, O Pericles! hast commanded me to adorn the temples of the gods. But not in executing alone; for, by Apollo, his own designs are so excellent, that I begin to feel more jealous of him than of Polycletus himself."

"And what," inquired Aspasia, "are the particular merits which thou discoverest in his productions?"

"I had almost answered," he replied, "that his works have all the perfections which sculpture ought, or is able to exhibit. But I think that he is especially remarkable for the life and eager motion with which he seems to inspire figures in full youth and activity. He has lately wrought an Atalanta in clay, as graceful and airy as our young friend Dryope. And he alone has satisfied me by the groups of the Lapithæ and Centaurs, which he has added to those designed by myself."

"A mighty praise!" said the mistress of Pericles; "I should like to see thy Sicyonian wonder."

"That will be difficult," answered the master; "for he is wrapt up in his art; and I believe that, if I could induce him to steal an hour from the chisel, and to visit thee, he would see, even in thyself and Dryope, no more than models to be studied and copied."

"And dost thou think," she asked, "that there would be nothing for a woman to be vain of, in supplying so accomplished an artist as this Cydon with examples for his nymphs and goddesses? Thou shalt bring him hither tomorrow. If he will speak of nothing else, he shall rave the eloquent mysteries of his art, until we believe that Destiny, and Night, and Heaven, the earliest Powers, were mighty sculptors, and that in statuary alone are to be found the true harmony and purpose and ideal model of human existence."

The morrow and its evening came, and brought Cydon to the house of Aspasia. The day and hour was unpropitious to the sculptor. He had before been indifferent to all things but his own pursuit. Engaged in it he had been tranquil, cheerful, happy. He was now thrown among those, who to a relish for the arts as lively, if not so deep and devoted, as his own, added eloquence and wit and beauty, and noble and winning manners, and a thousand accomplishments. At first he was surprised and bewildered, then dazzled, then delighted, then seduced. The Dryope, whose name has before been mentioned, was younger than Aspasia, and a native of her own Miletus. Pleased by the fresh and simple spirit of the young sculptor, and amused by the wondering eagerness with which he enjoyed those pleasures of society he had never known before, she bestowed a degree of attention and favour on him, which many of the wealthiest and greatest men in Athens could neither purchase nor command. Is it strange that Cydon should have been gratified, attracted, overpowered? His sacred enthusiasm for his divine art was laid asleep. His love of ideal beauty haunted him no more. It seemed to him that keenness and reality had been wanting in the most cherished of his past enjoyments.

The effect of his new state of mind on the productions of his chisel soon became visible. The simple severity, the harmonious unity, which had before distinguished his designs, disappeared; and his statues began to address themselves to the vulgar eye, to the senses, to the passions, the excitement of which precludes the pleasures of the imagination, and the love of the consistent, the abstract, the austerely beautiful. Aspasia smiled, while Phidias sighed, at the disease, the madness of Cydon. He meanwhile, uninitiated in the schools of philosophy, and accustomed to reflect on nothing but the laws of outward grace and perfection, knew not his own temper or condition. He felt that his calmness, his self-reliance, his reverence for his art were diminished or destroyed; but he knew not why. He cherished a vehement and almost delirious passion for Dryope: but he could not explain why it was, that, in the intervals of mental excitement, he was overpowered by an aching discontent.

After a few months of this fluctuating and painful existence, his temper became uncertain; and his intellectual vivacity broke forth only in fits, which were commonly followed by pauses of sullen silence, or by bursts of bitter sarcasm against himself and all mankind. Dryope began to treat him with disdainful coldness, or ridicule, half playful, half severe; and at last Cydon determined to reassert his former self-command, and went to the house of Aspasia, where he expected to meet Dryope, for the purpose of bidding her farewell. She was not there. Her lover was angry at himself and her, and sat mute and apart. But Socrates, who delighted to cope with all men in their strangest moods, and who was then young and adventurous, placed himself beside the sculptor, and began to converse with him in his unostentatious method, so singularly fit for concealing his design and for obtaining its accomplishment. Their dialogue was long and various; and till near its conclusion Cydon did not suspect that it had any particular reference to his state of mind. But, when the philosopher arose and bade him good evening, he began to consider the purport of all they had been saying; and he found that the causes and nature of the delusive temptations to which he had for months been yielding, were laid open before him with a clearness of which he had no previous experience. Self-reproach and the resolution of amendment divided his soul; and he left the house of Aspasia in many respects an altered man.

The evening had closed in, when Cydon began to walk alone and moody in the outskirts of Athens. He mused with sorrow on his wasted days and lost tranquillity; and the thoughts as to the origin and destiny of man, which had been excited in him by the conversation of Socrates, revived and gained augmented power. His gloomy meditations and doubts were suddenly interrupted, when he found himself in the neighbourhood of a vast multitude gathered around and beneath a grove of trees, which appeared as mere masses of uncertain shadow in the deepening twilight. Throughout the crowd there was a hum and stir of expectation. Cydon pressed among them, in the hope of making his way to the other side of an assemblage, in which he felt no interest: but he soon found himself one of the innermost ring of spectators, who encompassed a large level space in the centre of the grove.

Near him stood an altar, on which priests and elders were offering sacrifice. After a few minutes proclamation was made in a loud voice, that whoever wished to take part in the sacred torch-race should come forward. About twenty young men presented themselves, and threw off their mantles. To each of them a torch was given. When the last had been supplied, Cydon fancied that he heard a clear, steady whisper at his ear, saying, "Thou too, O Cydon! must engage in the torch-race, and struggle for the prize." He could not account for the violence of the impulse, which led him to lay aside his cloak, and range himself among the competitors. A moment's delay had taken place; and the people shouted their joy, when in the light of the altar they saw another candidate step forward and ask for a torch.

The runners were ranged in line. A flame at a distance was pointed out to them as the goal round which they were to pass, and so return to the altar; and each was then desired to kindle his torch at the sacred fire. One prayed to Jupiter, another to Venus, a third to Pallas, a fourth to the Dioscuri. Cydon prayed not at all; but he sighed to think how little even Dryope would now care to hear of his success. While this thought was passing through his mind, he seemed to hear the same unknown voice, which had before addressed him, exclaim, "O! Fire, which didst first give life to the soul of man, be thou propitious to Cydon." He started and looked hastily round; but he could only see the sharp lights and deep masses of shadow amid the band of priests and rivals, and the red and flitting gleams on a few of the thousands of earnest faces that encircled him. The stars were still dim above; and the sky appeared to weigh with a load of darkness on the assembly.

In another instant the signal had been given; and the runners, bearing the torches in their hands, had sprung forward on their course. He who first returned to the altar with his torch still burning, was to be the conqueror. The troop rushed on, gleaming and flashing, like a rout of phantoms, each armed with a meteor. The voices of the multitude broke forth into a wild shout as they burst away; and then succeeded a breathless silence, while the spectators attempted to make out the fate of each competitor. One by one the torches were seen to be extinguished: and before they had reached the turning point, the numbers were reduced to less than half of those which had begun the race. But to the persons round the altar the excitement of the spectacle was much augmented; for the faces of the youths were now visible; and every instant brought them nearer to the goal. The rapid limbs were at first scarcely discernible; but the lights blazed on the eager countenances, and, as they glanced along, threw a momentary glare on the pressing line of spectators, who, as soon as the contending racers passed by, closed in like a wave of the sea behind them. At length but two candidates remained. The foremost panted violently, but covered his mouth with his hand, lest his breathing should agitate the flame. They were now hard by the altar; and the hinder of the rivals had but a second for his final effort. With a long bound he passed his antagonist, whose torch was extinguished in the same moment by the rush of air. As to the first at the goal, and to him whose torch had alone remained unextinguished, the prize was adjudged to Cydon. The multitude shouted again, as if for an Athenian victory, at the triumph of one whose name scarcely ten among them had ever heard before.

The youth escaped as speedily as possible from the crowd, and took his way through the most gloomy and retired portion of the grove. When he had reached a spot of almost entire darkness, he leaned against the stem of a large plane-tree, and began to meditate, what, why, and whence he was, by what laws called on to guide himself, and destined to what end.

"Knowest thou," said the low and piercing voice, which he had twice heard already that evening, "knowest thou in what solemnity thou hast been engaged, and victorious?" Surprised and awestruck as Cydon was, he had scarcely courage to answer; and before he could say "No," the voice continued: "The altar in this grove is sacred to Prometheus, to the Titan who animated man by fire from heaven. In his honour those torches were kindled, and the prize instituted which was won by thee It is thy destiny to seek out the cave, in which the flame, brought by him from the sun, is still burning. Frame, as thou art skilled, a woman; and enliven her with that immortal fire. So shall thy happy fate be accomplished; and so shall I be freed."

Cydon became a wanderer on the earth. In the midst of solitudes, at the depth of night, that startling and mournful voice had come to him, and told him that the release of the warning spirit from its misery depended on his success in discovering the cave of Prometheus, and in achieving the task assigned to him. The weary and painful enterprise more than once disgusted the sculptor. He turned aside from his lonely pilgrimage, and plunged into the crowds of cities. His journeying in the deserts of the world had not indeed given him the knowledge of the spot he was in search of; but he had often carelessly collected golden ingots pure from the rude native moulds of the rocks, and in wastes marked with the footsteps of the lion, and crevices inhabited by serpents, had gathered caskets of beryl and emerald. With these he had the means of displaying royal state, and purchasing unbounded pleasures; but at the moments when his soul was about to sink into vanity and self-indulgence, he was scared and roused by that pursuing voice. He appeared for an instant in a popular assembly, a way-worn citizen in a foreign garb: but in the tumult that followed his first solemn and menacing words, the unfailing voice came shrill and commanding to his ear; and he turned and fled. Nor was it clearly determined afterwards, whether he had been a messenger from the guardian deities of the city, or a criminal haunted by the Furies. He rushed into a field of battle, and broke violently through a phalanx of spears; and when he was hailed as meriting the prize of valour, by those whom he had recklessly aided, a whisper overpowered the crash of arms and clang of trumpets, and compelled him to resume his solitary and dreary travels.

"I too," pronounced the voice, "was myself, like thee, the foremost in the torch-race. I too undertook this enterprise: but I was turned aside by folly and weakness. Ages have passed away; and I am still a miserable wanderer: nor can I be released from my suffering but by thy success; and if thou shalt yield to any delusive temptation, and forego the task thou hast entered on, such as is my destiny, such will be thine."

Seven years of watching and labour and fruitless hope had been spent by Cydon since the night he departed from Athens. He found himself at last in the midst of loftier and wilder eminences than any he had before seen. Masses of rock and sharp crags showed themselves on all sides among thickets and patches of rank herbs. Above, the breasts of the mountains rose immensely, distinct with various shades of barrenness; and the ice-peaks and frozen precipices towered over all, white, green, azure, and sparkling. Down an abrupt ravine a cataract tumbled and roared, and, from the point where Cydon stood, was only discernible by the smoke-like vapour and foam that hung in a wavering cloud over the black and solid phalanx of pine-trees. A sheer, immeasurable descent, dark with foliage, lay at his feet; and far below, through a cleft of the hills, the grey straight line of the ocean was faintly visible. The distant vultures were flying heavily, like slow specks in the air, around their desolate haunts; and the rustling of the forest reached his ear, mingled with the echoing howl of beasts of prey.

But the wanderer turned from the prospect before him, and examined a natural archway, under the shadow of which he was standing. It was the mouth of a cavern, the roof of which lifted itself to a vast height, and which extended far into the mountain. To him who was placed beneath it, and who was looking outwards, it appeared like some great proscenium, through which might be beheld a scene of awful savageness and immensity. The depth of gloom within defied all scrutiny of the eye; and Cydon felt a trembling eagerness and solemn wonder, while he thought that he had now perhaps arrived at the spot which was to be the term of his journeyings, and which was so much more important to him than any other on earth. He offered up a silent prayer to the mighty powers whose sanctuary he had approached; and after bathing in the waters of a spring, that rose on the threshold of the cave and then flowed down the mountain, he prepared to penetrate into the furthest recesses of that dark solitude.

He did not dare to supply himself with a torch; for he knew that no earthly fire must approach the spot where the flame of heaven burnt. A few paces therefore brought him into complete night. The walls of rock were drawn more closely together; the pathway descended rapidly; and the Athenian pursued his journey through those unknown depths with blind but cautious intrepidity. He had advanced a great distance, when he heard a rush of waters sounding as if below him. By feeling around he discovered that he was on the edge of a chasm; and balancing himself on the extreme verge, and stretching forward to the utmost, he touched a barrier of stone, which, if he had been on the other side of the abyss, would have prevented all further progress. He had no choice therefore, but either to return or to descend into the cleft. He did not hesitate long. Hanging by his hands on the brink, he let down his feet, and reached a narrow and uncertain resting-place. The rude natural wall, down which he was climbing, descended further than the deepest well ever excavated by man; and Cydon was constantly in the most imminent danger of perishing. At length, by the increasing loudness of the water, he knew that he had to encounter a different peril. He touched the stream with his feet, determined either to wade or swim across it; but the violence of the torrent rendered either plan impracticable; and being desperately resolved to perform what he had undertaken, or die, he leaped in the black darkness, with the hope of attaining the other side. He fell in the water, but soon reached the stony bank; and thence, through a long maze of winding passages, he pursued his way, till, on turning round a sharp angle in the rock, he saw the cavern he had sought, and the sacred fire.

The place was an immense hall, in the centre of which the flame was burning, raised on no altar, nor fed with any fuel, but hanging at the height of a man's knee above the bare granite floor. It was of the size and brightness of the noon-day sun, but of a more irregular form and wavering splendour. An immeasurable vista of rock stretched on all sides; and when Cydon came in sight of the subterranean luminary, he had still a long journey before he could reach it. No relic, no monument, no inscription on the eternal cliffs and vast expanse of stone, recorded that this had been the retreat and workshop of the Titan. The flame itself was a sufficient evidence; and when the Athenian drew near to it, he bowed to the ground, and, amid the boundless and lonely silence that surrounded him, heard the quick throbbings of his own awe-stricken bosom.

He believed himself under the guidance of a wonderful destiny. With equal labour, but less of anxiety than before, he retraced his way to upper earth and the light of day; but he found at his return that it was already midnight; and weary and happy he sank to sleep.

Cydon determined that thenceforth the outer cavern should be his abode, and the spot sacred to his labours. From the woods around he brought the materials for a couch of moss and leaves, which he laid in a recess at one side of the gigantic chamber. The fountain supplied him with his only and sufficient beverage. The thickets and brakes of the valleys abounded in wild fruitage and various kinds of nuts; and in these he was to find his food. He armed himself with a knotty staff, sufficient in his youthful and vigorous hands to slay all but the fiercest and most powerful of the savage animals; and with their skins he purposed to clothe himself. Thus prepared in all necessary respects for his future life, the Athenian began to range over those solitary valleys, and to climb the rugged precipices.

He sought on all sides for the means requisite to the fulfilment of his enterprise; and wandering far and boldly in an unknown land, he was often benighted at a distance from the cave, and saw the stars rise from a sea on which no sail ever glided, or cross the gap of sky over some narrow gorge, which no human steps had before trodden. After the search and labour of months, he succeeded in collecting a mass of iron ore. With his own hands he built a furnace, and heaped the branches of wood which were to feed its fire. Thus he obtained steel sufficient to construct tools and weapons; and he rejoiced to have made so long a stride towards accomplishing his design.

When once or twice, during these months of toil, his hand and resolution for a moment failed him, he was startled and warned from the forest by the groans of his invisible pursuer; and thus urged, he resumed his labour, and so far successfully performed it.

He again began to search the wilderness for those of its productions which were needful to him. From the banks of streams, and from nooks on the rocky shore of the ocean, he gathered the purest sands, the whitest and smoothest clay. Among the mountains he obtained fragments of the most transparent alabaster, and every metal that enriches the coffers in the dark, antique treasuries of the earth. With these materials he began to plan the work. During many days and nights a shadow appeared to flit around him, which perpetually mocked his grasp, and changed its aspect. For a moment he thought he had sight of the image which he was called on to embody; but before he could fix on it a steady gaze, it turned into the smiling and voluptuous form of Dryope; and then it seemed that she too departed, and left only the spectral and invisible presence of the unknown being who had so often warned and excited him.

When unable to gain the idea he was searching for, he recurred to all the sculptured or living beauty he had ever seen, in the faint hope of constructing the form for which he longed from these recollections. But each confused or effaced the others; and in no single image of his memory did he find the characteristics he required. At last he was wearied out by many efforts, and fevered by fruitless anxiety. Absorbed and harassed by his thoughts, he had long forgotten to supply himself with needful sustenance; and he sank exhausted on the rocky floor of the cavern. The wide entrance grew dark with night; and slowly and painfully he became aware that figures were shaping themselves in light on the dusky groundwork. They passed along the sky in gliding procession, with the swift and easy pace of dreams. First came the stately Cybele, and then a group of queens with diadems, laureled priestesses, and prophetic virgins bearing the lyre. To these succeeded the wild mountain women of Arcadia and Thessaly, strangely clothed, some armed like hunters, some wielding the implements of sorcery. They were followed by a band of captive maidens, weeping and chained, the spoil of a city, — and these by a giddy troop of Bacchantes, striking high their cymbals and tambourines, waving branches laden with purple grapes, leading the leopard and the young lion in leashes of vine-boughs, and mingled with laughing children, and pursued by reeling fauns. A space of darkness divided them from a company of Spartan mothers, attired as they were wont to be for the festivals of their mythology. But the last figures of the train were far less grave and matronly than those who preceded them, and could scarcely be distinguished from the foremost shapes in a knot of those beautiful singers and flute-players and dancers, whom Cydon had seen before. They turned their eyes on him; and he fancied for an instant that he recognised the features and look of Dryope, when they all faded away. Soon on the dim void a stern, gigantic shadow moved along, with his left hand pressed upon his heart, where the vengeance of Jove had struck, and his right uplifted as if in fixed and triumphant resolution. It was the form of Prometheus. Behind him glided Mercury the life-giver, and Pallas; and between them Cydon beheld a lovely being, the image he so long had sought. An earnest calm, a youthfulness as if from the land of the morning, pervaded the lovely phantom, and inspired the rapt artist.

With a glad spirit and hopeful confidence Cydon began his labour. The waters of the fountain, the salt waves of the sea, fire and sunlight, and the animating air were all employed by him to purify or melt or mingle the materials he had collected. The flame which he had kindled under the arch of the cavern, and fed with branches of pine and oak, blazed nightly like a beacon, unbeheld by any eyes but his, and, to him when returning belated from his search for food, seemed glowing with a strange glare, and as if it might well have gathered around it a wild company of robbers, and fair forest witches, and horned satyrs. By these toils he at last succeeded in obtaining the pure and beautiful substance, of which the new offspring of his art and mistress of his soul was to be framed. It united the whiteness and polish of the pearl, and might have been thought akin, like it, to the spray of the ocean, from which the goddess of beauty rose, and whose mighty and secret spirit was the parent of Prometheus.

The artist drew no design, and shaped no model: possessed by the vision he had seen, he found his only and sufficient rule in it. Slowly and reverentially he attempted to realize it in his work; and he trembled like a votary who handles the most awful symbols of his religion, while he smoothed and adapted the plates, as thin and delicate as layers of the finest shell, or steeped them in the transparent waters, or softened them with gentle heat. From the first hours of his labour he felt as if the imperfect shape had been animated by a sentient consciousness, could mourn and reproach him for a moment's neglect, and long like him for the completion of his task. Therefore with a beating heart he daily flew, at the instant of his waking, to the mute idol of his worship; and the freshness of the morning air, the singing of the birds, the sunshine tempered by the winds and by the overarching rock, and the beautiful expanse of landscape gave him a new pleasure, from a faint but constant feeling of sympathy between him and the fair image of his hands. He often pursued his occupation till long after the moon had risen between the hills. The red light of the fire shone on the projecting crags; and the pale rays of the luminary beamed unbroken on the statue, which glittered as if of more exquisite substance than silver or ivory; while a low murmur breathed from the forest, the fountain whispered at his feet, and it even seemed to Cydon that a dreamy song came from the stars and ocean, and was inly repeated by the shape, at the perfecting of which he so devoutly toiled. While the spirit-like light of Heaven was reflected by the polished limbs and bosom, and the glory was only interrupted by the moving shadow of the sculptor's head and hands, he felt as if engaged in an act purer, less earthly, and holier, than had ever before presented itself to his thoughts. The shape gained splendour and a celestial life from the beams which illumined it, and which almost belonged as a natural halo to the still severity, the innocent youthfulness, the composed lightness, and winning dignity of its aspect.

Yet, even when the work was on the point of being completed, the long continuance of labour, and the depression which follows extreme joy, had nearly withdrawn Cydon from his appointed task. The image of Dryope still haunted him in the flush of her youthful, seductive beauty; and the sculptor was at last so maddened by the memory of his early passion, and the loveliness of the vision, that he was rushing to pursue her, when the melancholy cry of the unseen warder rang from the woods below. The delusive shape vanished from his eyes, and returned no more.

Seven years had passed since Cydon reached the cave. The figure was perfected; and he looked on his fair achievement with a passionate yet religious love. He threw himself on the ground before it, and gazed at it for hours. The one hand drooped in front; the other was half extended from the bosom, and raised to the level of the head. A tranquil smile slept on the lips; and the eyes which were bent towards him, looked as if waiting to beam with intelligence and affection. Such a creature might have glided from the evening star, and would have stood thus tranquil, thus exquisite, thus delicately pure, seeming, amid that dark rock, those gloomy woods, and that barbarous ruggedness of prospect, a being of a brighter and sublimer element than earth includes or man imagines.

"Soon, soon," exclaimed the Sculptor, "shall this white rose-bud open its leaves to the sunshine, breathe in the air of heaven, and tremble at my touch with life and love."

He hastily built an altar of stone before the image, and heaped precious gums on it and boughs of fragrant wood. He then framed a torch that would burn slowly and long;

and thus prepared he again descended into the earth. He encountered the same difficulties and dangers as before, and overcame them with equal courage. Again he reached the Hall of the Sun-Flame, which glowed as intensely as when he first saw it. He prayed to the genius of the place, and invoked the name of the Titan, and then with reverence and determination kindled his torch in that dazzling fire. The parent blaze died on a sudden; and its extinction was accompanied by an overpowering peal, which seemed to shake the primeval earth around him: but his torch still burned and lighted him on his way through the dark abysses of the world. He bore it across the river, and climbed the perilous ascent beyond. It still beamed in his hand when he reached the upper cave; and with trembling anxiety, in the darkness of the night, he applied it to the fuel on the altar. The flame rose bright and clear, a pillar of glory; but suddenly it broke and wavered, and seemed to cling and adapt itself to the limbs of the statue, which quivered as it were with the first thrill of life, and welcomed the light to its bosom. But the work of Cydon's hands dissolved and fell away, and disclosed the new and beautiful creature, to whom it had served as a husk or chrysalis. He too sank and expired. The last sound that pierced his ears, was a cry of joy from the forest, which told the relief of his pursuer. The last sight that filled his eyes, was the look of the ascending maiden, who, as she rose aloft into that starry sky, turned on him a look of affection, and beckoned his spirit to follow her from the earth.

Melita: A Fragment of Greek Romance

(From The Athenaeum, 1829)

Melita was a maiden of Elis; and no fairer spirit had ever inhabited that peaceful land. Her beauty was known but to few; for her mother had long been dead; and her father was the humble dweller in an obscure abode. She had neither brother nor sister, and had seldom been seen by any eyes but those of her aged parent. His well-ordered industry and serene affection surrounded her with a clear unchanging life; and she scarcely knew of any variation in the world, but day and night, autumn and spring, the gradual whitening of her father's hairs, and the growth and impulse of her own feelings. As she approached to womanhood, her thoughts began to overleap the low grassy mound, with which the narrow plat of her existence had previously been encircled, and on which, even from her infancy, many bright phantoms had appeared to her to stand in the morning sunshine. Her wishes now attempted to follow the unknown flight of those gay shadows; and she longed to resemble them in rising with the lightness of a bird over the boundary which divided her from the busy and glittering world. When Melita had reached her fifteenth year, the time came round for the celebration of the Olympic games. She heard from her father some short and broken accounts of the splendid festivals, at which he had frequently been present; and she was lost in bewildering excitement, while she fancied a succession of pageants led by glorious beings of whose forms she was utterly ignorant. But above all she was possessed by the resemblance, which she had wrought in her imagination, of the deity to whose honour these rites and contests had been instituted.

In the morning of the first day of the games, she almost unconsciously expressed, in her father's presence, her earnest longing to behold the bodily presence of the great Jupiter. The old man started out of his usual tranquillity of manner, and said to her, "Unhappy, my daughter, is the mortal to whom such a vision shows itself: he who has conversed with a god, is for ever unfitted to lead the life of earthly men. To eyes which long for the sight of superior natures, their desire is sometimes granted; but that for which they yearned is always fruitful of horror and destruction. I could tell you a prediction which your mother heard from the oracle; but . . . ." He said no more; for the time had approached at which the solemnities were to begin; and he hastily left the house.

This conversation did not diminish the uneasy mystery which filled the mind of Melita. All day she brooded over the thoughts which had occupied her; and, when her father returned in the evening, she was restless, eager, and confused. The dusk had come before his entry; and he had scarcely been able to speak to her, when a slight knock was heard, followed, as it seemed to them, by a faint groan. The old man turned the door on its sleepy hinges, and found a young man lying on the earth, who was evidently broken down by some malady. He lifted up the youth, and carried him into the house. The stranger was clothed in a remarkable dress, and appeared not more than eighteen. He was revived by the care of Melita and her father, but still continued feeble and suffering. They learned from his low and interrupted words, that he had come from one of the farthest Grecian islands, with the design of contending at the games for the prize of poetry. But he seemed almost delirious; and he told no connected tale. He remained for several hours pained in body and wandering in mind. Among other hints and ravings, he spoke some scattered phrases as to the magnificence and interest of the festivity, which he had seen on that day for the first time. He was then seized by the recollection of the ode which he had intended to recite on one of the subsequent days. The stanzas, which he murmured at intervals, were full of fervour, of religious awe, and splendid images, and belonged to a lyrical description of the intercourse of Jupiter with mortal maidens. Some of the fragments were so passionate and impressive, and Melita listened with an interest so full of wonder and rapt excitement, that her father commanded her to retire, and leave the patient under his care.

She lay awake for several hours, and at last fell asleep, with a brain and bosom possessed by tumultuous and gorgeous visions. Early in the morning her father announced to her that the youth had in the night become much calmer, and that he had left him to obtain some short repose. When she had arisen, the boy was no longer to be found; but he had left his rich and remarkable dress behind him, and had only taken away an old mantle, which had been thrown over him by his host, while he lay on the couch. Her father added that he was now about to join the crowd at the games, and that he should not return till late in the evening. She placed herself in the room in which the youth had lain, and employed herself in putting together all she could remember of his strange and imperfect phrases, and in connecting them with the wishes and fantastic images which had filled her mind before. Near to her lay the garments which he had worn. Melita fixed her eyes on them; and she felt as if some unseen enchantment prevented her from looking away, even for a moment. As the day closed in, the evening wind arose, and brought to her ears the distant applauses of the Grecian people gathered at their chief solemnity. She gazed and mused, and, after a struggle of fear, shame, curiosity, and vague wishfulness, could no longer resist the temptation. She hastily put on the dress of the poet, and left the house.

Her impetuous and winged feet bore her she knew not whither. In a short time she had moved a considerable distance, when she beheld a procession of worshippers, headed by the priests, and accompanied by many attendants. She joined their ranks, and was surprised to see that the youths in the service of the gods were clothed exactly as she was, so that she could pass without notice. The train advanced to the sacred grove which surrounded the Olympian temple; and here she beheld, with delight and astonishment, the long files of statues, which exhibited the conquerors at the games, with the emblems of the exercises in which they had triumphed. The evening light flowed beautifully through the interstices of the dark foliage, and fell with a soft illumination on the still and white heroic figures. The throng moved on; and, while the greater number placed themselves before the lofty and shadowy portico of the temple, a few of the priests and of their attendant boys entered the building. Among these Melita ventured to glide; and, from the instant which gave her a glimpse of the god, she was insensible to all else.

She sank on the marble pavement in the shade of the gigantic deity, and watched his form as intently as the astrologer watches the star on which his destiny depends. The twilight was broken by the thin flames of a few distant censers; and it seemed to her that she discerned the limbs and features of the statue rather by some radiance of their own than by any outward beam. The calm and mighty face was more beautiful than all she had imagined. The brow was girded with olive, and appeared a bright throne for heavenly supremacy; the deep eyes were filled with a solemn and a lovely spirit; and she felt that she should rejoice to breathe away her soul upon that mouth, so awful and yet so sweet. The gleam of dusky gold on the garments in which Jupiter was clad, gave the semblance of a faint and floating glory; but all that was in the temple of distinguishable light gathered on the celestial countenance, and kept it, even when night had almost closed without, a visible revelation of the greatest god.

The girl was startled amid her adoration by a voice appearing to come from beyond the portico, and singing the words of the hymn, snatches of which had been uttered by the poet in her father's house the day before. She thought, but could not be sure, that she recognised the same tones pronouncing the enthusiastic poetry of the ode which she had heard under such different circumstances; and they blended strangely with her own fearful ecstasy at the presence of the king of heaven. When this ode had been sung by a low but earnest voice, a single strophe of a different style and manner was vociferated in thundering music by the whole company of priests and novices. Scared by this overpowering sound, Melita shrank among the officiating train, and looked at the crowd of worshippers collected before the temple. She thought she recognised her father. Trembling and uncertain, she glided away; and, when she had gained the solitary wood, ran with all her speed through thickets of trees and groups of glimmering statues, which she feared were living pursuers; till, wearied and agitated, she reached her humble home. Her father speedily returned; but she had already changed her dress; and as soon as she had saluted him she retired to her chamber.

When she had thrown herself on her couch, she began to meditate on the occurrences of the last few hours. The hint of the oracular prediction, — the poet, with earnest tones, faint indeed and broken, but of exquisite sweetness, — the distant sounds of the multitude congregated around the stadium, — the long procession of priests and worshippers, with the garlands and the incense, — the green twilight of the consecrated grove, and the white gleam of those unmoving marble champions; — all these were present to her mind; but chiefly the murmuring stillness of the vast temple, with the wavering flashes from the tripods, cutting the evening gloom, and, over all, the form, whose ivory limbs were wrapt in a golden shadow, the noblest exhibition of deified humanity, the king, the god, the beautiful, the one master of her soul, Jupiter, the wonder of Greece, and glory of the earth, filled, overawed, agitated, and attracted her.

The deep dark night was around her; and she had remained for an hour absorbed in these contemplations, when suddenly a bright blaze started at once from the wall, the floor, and ceiling of the chamber, and covered them as if with a fiery drapery. It gave out no heat, but flamed with a steady and topaz-like lustre. Melita gazed in astonishment at the wondrous light, which did not however scare her with any resemblance of an earthly conflagration. It burned for a few seconds; and, when she had in some degree overcome her first alarm by perceiving the innocence of the lights, innumerable snakes of the most various colours appeared to move and float along the walls, and to play in the lucid blaze. Green and white, black and crimson, blue, purple, and orange, starred with jewels, and streaked like the tulip, they wove together, in that liquid illumination, a thousand knots and momentary devices. Arching themselves like the rainbow, or in ranks like some gorgeous oriental cavalry, they moved from the sides of the chamber to the ceiling, or twined around the simple furniture.

The serpents appeared to melt and mingle into each other, and were swallowed by the general splendour; and the burning boundaries of the room widened and receded, till they resembled the atmosphere of an evening sky, filled with the richest and most sparkling clouds. Amid these, as if disclosed from the burning disk of the sun, a large bird, of as brilliant plumage as the fabled Phoenix, flew forward, and passed before her. But soon it appeared to change its shape and lose its glory, and became a gigantic owl with round bright eyes. The evening prospect darkened into night: the white crescent of the moon stood over the shaded hills; and the grey bird perched on a rock which overhung the sea. The new moon in that world of witchery appeared to rise at nightfall, and for a moment she watched its silent ascent. A faint musical sound caused her to look away: on the rock where she had seen the owl alight, the young poet was now leaning. The sea glimmered at his feet; one arm rested on a projection of the crag; and his eyes were turned as hers had been to the diamond curve that adorned the darkness of the sky. She fancied that in his countenance she discovered a resemblance to the pale and majestic loveliness of that statue of Jupiter, which to her was far more than a statue. Clouds came over the heavens and obscured the view. The youth was no longer visible; but a dull twilight covered the foreground; and through this two small red stars were burning. She looked at them intently, and shuddered at discerning the form of a gigantic lion, couched, as it seemed, at a little distance from her, and watching her with the glowing eyes which had first drawn her attention. He seemed to grow nearer and nearer to her; and the whole picture had soon disappeared, leaving nothing but the shaggy monster and the dim and narrow room. The lion rose, and with a light bound laid himself on the bed before her feet. The enormous shape became less terrible, when she was within its reach; and while her foot appeared to touch its flank, and its mane lay spread on part of the mantle, which in her terror she had let fall from around her, she thought that it was no more than an enormous and threatening shadow.

When the chaotic dimness of the chamber was dispersing into the clear transparency of a summer night, Melita remembered the tales she had heard of Proteus and his wonders; and the bewilderment of her mind had little of terror or suffering. The desert-shape which shared her couch, rolled away amid the mist which now vanished from the room. Its fiery eye-balls seemed gradually to recede, till they were lost among the throng of stars that twinkled in the cloudless firmament. Wild troops of birds and insects fluttered around her; and trains of children, whose whispers were like distant tinklings, moved hither and thither bearing baskets of flowers. A pink light gradually spread through the air; and one of the children detached itself from the playful ring of its companions, and approached her. In that carnation splendour everything was hidden but the gentle, smiling boy, who seemed to walk on the charmed wind. His delighted eyes were fixed laughingly on her; and in another instant she had stretched her hands, and he was pressed to her uncovered bosom. She laid her head on the pillow; and he nestled in her arms, while she gazed with eager pleasure on the sunny locks that clustered round the brow of the infant, and strained to her side his round and rosy limbs.

But her countenance assumed a deeper meaning, and she trembled with emotion, when it seemed to her that the lines of that baby loveliness became stronger and more expressive, that the eye darkened and spoke earnestly to hers, and that the lips were pressed with more than childish passion on her quivering mouth; when she thought that in this young visitant she could recognise at every moment a nearer likeness to the island poet. But soon this resemblance also escaped from her. The forehead became more lovely, the features nobler and more radiant; the gleam, as of a golden cloak thrown off, was spread under his finely proportioned limbs; and now for the first time she perceived, among the dark brown hair, the slender olive-wreath, and in all the form and look, the well remembered presence of the Olympic god.

On the next morning, when the father of Melita was

leaving his house, he informed his daughter that the young stranger whom they had aided, was on that day to be crowned as the successful poet. Scarcely had he departed, when, seized with an impetuous frenzy, she rushed away to the place where the festival was held. The poet had not appeared; and the prize was given to the second of the competitors. But it was a deadly crime in any woman to approach the spot; and Melita, before the eyes of all the people, and of her white-haired father, was precipitated from a rock into the river Alpheus; such being the punishment appointed from of old for her offence.

"Heavily, O my daughter!" said the aged man, "have the maxims of the wise, and the prediction of the oracle been fulfilled in thee!"

The Lycian Painter

(From The Athenaeum, 1829)

Nicon, king of Lycia, had become celebrated in all Asia Minor for his skill and valour as a military commander, and his wisdom and justice as a ruler; and the waters of the Mediterranean, in which his palace was reflected, were daily traversed by vessels from distant lands, bringing merchants, suppliants, sages, and ambassadors to the throne of the king. He had passed the middle period of life, when his queen died. The corpse was laid on a bier in the hall of the palace; and the subjects of the king assembled to honour the funeral. Flowers were thickly strewn; and loud cries of lamentation burst from the multitude, mingled with the groans of Nicon, and the sobs of his daughter Cleone, and his son Phineus. At the same time, in the pauses of the shrieks and wailings, a low and constant song was heard to be murmured, which sounded like a mixture of threats and prophecies; but no one could catch the import of the words, or knew the language to which they belonged. All were silent, and turned their eyes in the direction of the spot from which the song seemed to proceed. Its tones became wilder and more vehement; and the crowd shrank from a part of the vast room; and trembling fingers were pointed to a dim recess in the wall. In this the outline of a female figure was faintly visible. It began to move; and the singer came forward with slow steps, which gradually quickened as her song grew swollen and hurried. Her face was almost covered by a thick veil which shaded her brow, and by a mantle raised high above her bosom. But her eyes were seen to glance fiercely round the apartment, and at the king and his children, and sometimes glared with a look of triumph at the unmoving and covered body. Still the Mænad measure and the frenzied chaunt went on. When she came near any of the spectators, they started from her as if she had been a panther from the wilderness, or a gliding serpent. She had nearly gone round the room, when she approached the bier. She took from under her veil a chaplet of dark leaves which she had worn, and was about to fling it among the garlands heaped upon the pall, when Nicon rushed to her and seized her arm. She fixed her eyes on him for an instant, and shook off his grasp; and, while he sank upon a seat, she threw down the gloomy wreath, and for several moments sang at the fiercest pitch of her deep voice. Her long dark hair fell almost to her feet; and she whirled round in a frightful ecstasy, which seemed impelled by a stronger and more terrible spirit than that of our earthly nature.

Thus she rushed through the throng, which scattered like leaves before the north-wind; and in another instant she was gone. Before she disappeared, every garland but her own had withered; and, when they raised the pall, the beautiful corpse had shrunk and faded into a sallow mummy.

Months passed away; and on the bridal day of Cleone, a tall and dark-eyed woman approached the palace, sitting in a sculptured and gilded car, drawn by sable steeds, nobler than any in Lycia. She gave magnificent gifts to the bride; and the king received as a princess the visitor who brought so many evidences of her power and rank. It was observed however that he sometimes trembled under her look; and his attendants whispered, that the proud and fearless Nicon had never before been seen to quail in any human presence, except that of the stranger who had appeared at the funeral of his wife. That evening, in the midst of the rejoicing, Cleone died. The kingdom was filled with lamentations. But ere many weeks it was called on to make merry at the marriage of its sovereign with Mycale. She was of a stately beauty, which few men loved to look upon; and she was conspicuous for the haughtiness of her air, and the boldness with which she guided her black coursers among the mountains, and along the margin of the sea. A thousand rumours were uttered; and it was said that in a night of tempest she had been seen on the highest tower of the palace, her dark hair streaming round her and the lightning innocently flashing on her brow. Her song, it was reported, had been heard in the pauses of the gale; dark or fiery shapes had echoed it from the clouds; and she had saluted them with uplifted hands. However this may have been, it cannot be questioned that she collected round her a troop of bold retainers, and that their captain, a beautiful barbarian from the mountains, who had been the leader of a predatory band, the terror of Asia, and through her influence had been pardoned by Nicon, was now said to be her paramour.

At a great religious festival, the king, in the presence of all the people, suddenly flung off his diadem, overthrew the altar, and by his gestures and speech was evidently a fierce maniac. Phineus was still a boy; and Mycale obtained the supreme power. She confined her stepson in a small apartment, looking out on an enclosed garden, and never let him be seen by those whom he would be called upon to govern. But the frenzy of Nicon was ostentatiously displayed; and the horror of his subjects was frequently excited by the exhibition of the strangest and most lawless insanity.

Phineus lived a melancholy prisoner. His mind was filled with reflections on his dead mother and his maniac father. But above all he thought of his lovely and beloved sister, who had perished so suddenly and fearfully. As he sat in his solitary chamber, or cultivated the flowers of his narrow garden, and fed himself with the murmur of the sea, which was hidden from his eyes, the constant attendant on his hopeless plans and miserable recollections was the image of Cleone. He brooded over her memory, till at last it became so vivid that he must needs give it an outward expression. He endeavoured to paint a portrait of his sister.

Many days were employed in labouring, effacing, and again delineating, while the lines and colours maddened him by their feebleness and insufficiency; and many nights he lay awake, cherishing his recollection of the beautiful maiden, and comparing it in thought with the faint ineffectual form, which alone he had been able to create. The longing to accomplish his purpose became the master passion of his mind. In the shapes of trees and clouds his eyes traced out only the lines which bore some relation to those he wished to express in his picture. The colours of the world, the rays of light had scarcely any interest for him save that which they derived from their resemblance to the hues of his pencil. But still every effort was baffled; and the thousand imperfect shapes which he successively evoked, seemed all alike to exist for no other end than to mock and torment him. The disgust at the imperfection of each attempt added eagerness to the labour with which he destroyed it, and sought to substitute another. In the course of the many months which were occupied in this work, he was tempted innumerable times to give it up in despair. But the haunting image of Cleone returned to him amid his relaxations and his dreams, with so bright and living an aspect of reality, that he started from his idle mood, or rushed from his couch at midnight, and again with tremulous and burning fingers drew an outline, which his heart told him would prove as inadequate as all its predecessors. He tried to represent the maiden in her bridal dress, with jewels sparkling on her neck, and a garland of white violets around her hair; but the eyes so full of love and gentleness, the flushed cheek, the form bending with emotion, like a lily bowed by the weight of its own beauty, — how weak and rude, compared with his memory of these, was all that he could ever portray!

He commonly laboured in a room, the door of which was left open, and showed the corridor without, and beyond it the tranquil and flowery garden. When his exhausted heart and failing hand would no longer sustain the labour he imposed upon them, and his eyes were wearied of that chaos of colour from which he had been toiling to educe what for him was a universe, — he looked from the tablet and the walls which he was weary of beholding, to the clear deep air of heaven, and the little realm of silent life, which was filled with his bushes and blossoms, and peopled only by the wren and the butterfly. To this prospect his eyes were turned, after an attempt at painting so unsuccessful that he at last burst into tears. The evening had sailed along the sky, and steeped the earth in silvery twilight; and the stars were glittering brightly above the cypresses, poplars, and holm-oaks, which hid the garden wall. Amid these constellations it appeared to him that a patch of air became suddenly darker and more definite. It moulded itself into shape and colour; and Phineus beheld his sister. The form was indeed Cleone, growing like a fair plant out of the heavens, and surrounded by the radiance of the quiet stars. She seemed to be imbued with their splendour; the last light of sunset was on her cheek; and her aerial locks were still surrounded by the wreath of pearly violets. Her eyes were fixed on him; and gradually she seemed to detach herself from the empyrean, and approach nearer to the earth. She floated in the middle air; and he thought her garments were faintly stirred by the breeze which he heard cooing among the trees beneath her. When he would have called to her, she seemed to shrink back towards the sky, and to diminish from his view. But when he gazed at her with serene and motionless delight, she grew forth again into definite, though still visionary, beauty, till he almost believed that her feet, white and filmy as wandering gossamer, touched the topmost foliage of the dark trees in his garden.

He looked for many minutes; and he persuaded himself that the eyes of Cleone glanced for an instant from his face to the tablet from which he had just effaced her portrait. He seized his pencil, and renewed his labour, with all the earnestness of the enchanter in framing the talisman, which is to give him immortal youth, wealth without end, and power without limits. Every moment he lifted his eyes to heaven; and still Cleone was before him. His work brightened beneath his hand; and the lamp which burned beside him, seemed to emit a clearer and more genial light than ever before. He had wrought for a considerable time, when the moon rose: as its light pervaded the atmosphere, the figure dissolved into air. That night, the first for many months, Phineus slept calmly and happily; and in the morning he awoke refreshed. His painting appeared to him more faithful, brilliant, and expressive, than he had ever dreamed of making it. He refrained from using his pencil, for fear a touch might injure the magic woof he had already woven, and in a fearful, passionate hope that the vision might be renewed. All day he passed in his garden: his flowers had never appeared to him so exquisite, nor the sound of the waves so pregnant with music. He looked long at the region of the sky in which his sister had appeared to him; but nothing was visible except the bright blue depths filled with sunshine, traversed by silken fragments of thin cloud, or skimmed by glancing birds. He placed his painting in the corridor; and a thousand times, while he lay upon the grass, and imbibed the transparent noontide, he turned his eyes upon the tablet which bore so precious and potent a record of the vision of the previous evening. As the day closed in, his thoughts became more and more anxious; and, when at last the sun had set, no racer at the games ever stood prepared to start with a look of keener expectation, or with the blood coursing more wildly through his limbs, and eddying more hotly at his heart. Again, at the same spot of heaven, and encircled by the same constellations, Cleone was visible. The moon rose later than before; and till its disk appeared Phineus toiled delightedly at the picture. The third night she appeared again; and, when the dimness of the air began to brighten in the moonshine, he thought that her face grew sad, and that, by a slight gesture of the hand and head, she indicated that she would appear no more. With a sigh he dropped his pencil, as she melted into the heavens; and for some moments he forgot that the picture was now completed, and that it displayed his sister even more perfectly and intensely beautiful than he had ever seen her when on earth.

The celestial figure had not vanished long, when a storm arose, and the moon was hidden in darkness. He turned from the agony of the elements without, and gazed upon that adored image, which had power to withdraw his heart from everything but the contemplation of its own loveliness, and the innumerable happy remembrances connected with it. But his attention to the outward world was soon excited; for it seemed to him that in a brief pause of the tempest, he heard the well-remembered voice of Mycale chanting her wild incantations. With a shudder he crept to the corridor, and looked into the garden; and he beheld the queen, surrounded by those cypresses and cedars which were less black than the atmosphere, triumphing in a frenzied dance beneath the drowning rain, and her black hair, writhing features, and fierce gestures, illumined at intervals by the glare of lightning. Sometimes her song went forth in screams, accompanying the loudest fury of the whirlwind; and she stretched her hands, and bared her throbbing bosom to the blast, and the dim torrent of waters. Anon she stooped like some agile beast of prey, and plucked from the drenched sod various plants of necromantic virtue; and again she started into a whirling dance, and muttered threats in which Phineus thought he could distinguish his own name, and shook her uplifted hand as if against him.

He shrunk away in horror; and through all the night the sounds of the tempest bore to his ears the accents of the terrible enchantress. His terror ended in stupefaction; and, when he unclosed his eyes, wild yells were still ringing around him. But after a moment's pause he discovered that these were the expressions of his father's insanity, and not of the vengeance of Mycale. The king approached his chamber; and he heard his own name mingled with the curses and ejaculations which broke from the lips of the madman. In another instant the door was burst open; and Nicon hurried into the chamber with a dagger in his hand; his limbs were dropping blood from wounds he had himself inflicted. He was rushing to the couch on which his son had sunk, when his eye was caught by the picture of Cleone. The lamp was still burning beside it in the darkness. The maniac knew the form of his daughter, — and the dagger fell from his grasp. He looked intently on the lovely and innocent maiden; and, when his son approached him, he had fallen on his knees before her, and had clasped his forehead with his hands. His senses returned to him; and ere long the boy whom he had come to murder, was pressed by his embrace, and their tears were mingled. Mycale now entered the room, followed by her guards, and the beautiful savage warrior, her minion, and their commander. The first objects that met her eyes, were the picture of Cleone, and the father and son supporting each other beside it. The change that came over her form and features, rendered her a loathsome and horrible realization of all that we think of as most depraved; and when she commanded her followers to seize Nicon and Phineus, her lover flung away his sword, and fled from the palace to his native mountains; while the guards pointed through the open doorway to the sky, where they exclaimed that, amid the skirts of the receding tempest, the original of the heavenly form in the picture looked at them with a sad and awful aspect, which plucked the weapons from their grasp. None of them however had courage to arrest Mycale, who with a sneer of defiance walked through their array, and was no more seen.

The picture of Cleone was dedicated to Nemesis, and remained for many ages in the temple of the avenging Deity.

The Crystal Prison

(From Arthur Coningsby, 1833)

There was a Tartar Khan, one of whose favourite retainers, a young man of great beauty, fled in disguise from his service, rather than marry an ill-featured woman; and left behind him the distich,

> Beauty ought no more to unite with ugliness,
> Than the bird of Paradise with the night-owl.

He was pursued and overtaken; and the Khan determined to inflict upon him the severest punishment. For this purpose, by the advice of a dervish, he caused a chamber to be constructed, the walls, roof, and floor of which were mirrors of thick crystal; and the only light admitted came through openings concealed from the view of any one within. At night an artificial radiance, the source of which was concealed, illuminated the dungeon.

Here the prisoner was confined. Wherever he turned his eyes, he could see nothing but his own image. Around, above, below, everything was still the same agonizing self. He sometimes thought he would dare and stand the sight, and fixed his gaze on some one point, which presented the reflection of his unmoving countenance. Gradually he saw the features shrink, the glance waver; and he closed his eyelids, and shut out the stare of the remorseless avenger. But, as if he had been in the presence of a spectre, another moment forced him to look upon the image again. He shuddered at the terrible reality of the shadow; and, while his eyes wandered away, ravening for a resting-place, but despairing to find one, they encountered on all sides a thousand repetitions of their former misery.

In his sleep he at first gained some instants of repose. But gradually the face which he dreaded grew more and more distinct in his dreams, and multiplied to a sea. He woke with a scream, to find them glaring in myriads around him; or, if he riveted his look on one of the shapes, there was his own affrighted, self-petrifying visage, in all its steady outward truth. What would he not have given to be wrapt in darkness! How much more precious to him than the cup of water to the traveller in a desert, would have been a single spot of blankness, which he might have looked at and seen nothing! For him all the universe was concentrated into one tormenting form, and that his own. The most momentary look of commencing quiet, the faintest shiver of horror, every change of line or hue, all was flung back upon his heart from those encircling hell-walls. He tore his countenance with his hands to efface the hated lineaments; and still he was pursued by his own bloody and writhing features. Like light augmented into a blaze by innumerable reflectors, his agony was returned to him a million-fold; and its last result was madness and blindness.

The Sons of Iron

(From Arthur Coningsby, 1833)

In a valley surrounded by impassable mountains of coal and iron-ore, lived a race of whom no notice has ever reached mankind, but in vague and uncertain tradition. They were iron men. Formed of that strong material, of large stature, and beautiful proportions, they had a strange and puzzling resemblance to the children of Adam, but were far superior to them in honesty and understanding, as well as in force and agility.

This stern and upright people called themselves Siderians; their patriarch was named Chalybs. From him they received what instruction they possessed, and what simple rules were necessary for their government. He said, that of his own origin he knew only this: he had a dim impression that he owed his existence to two venerable powers, called Siderus and Sterope, and that they had communicated to him, in the dawn of his consciousness, the laws that were to guide his race. Of these the most important were two; that they should always labour to increase the number of Siderians, and that they should never attempt to penetrate into the edifice in the centre of the valley, as their destruction would be the inevitable consequence.

This building was a tower of polished steel, without windows or any opening but a door, beside which hung an iron key, apparently designed to fit the key-hole. The injunction however of Chalybs had always prevented any attempt to apply it to the lock; and the tower remained unopened. Near it, and so disposed as to form a large circle, when regarded in connexion with the tower, several tall rough blocks of iron-stone rose from the ground, and wore an air of desolate and awful antiquity. At the other extremity of the diameter from the forbidden edifice, was a mass of more regular shape than the rest, presenting the dim resemblance of an old and gigantic man, seated on a rock, with mouldering arms and implements of vast size scattered on its base. In this the inhabitants of the valley had learnt to trace the sacred image of their unknown parent, Siderus.

Chalybs remembered that, on the first day of his existence, the mountain-basin was filled with tempest, through which the lightning streamed in torrents. He found himself, when he awoke, in a cavern, on the face of a cliff. As he moved his limbs and looked around, the air became clear and quiet; the lightning ceased to flash; and he arose and explored his dominions. These exhibited only an irregular plain of metalliferous soil, with a lake of molten iron, for ever bubbling and heaving, near the tower. The prospect was closed in on all sides by the mountains of ore and of inflammable mineral. At the foot of one of the hills, a bed of coal was burning, and supplied the first Siderian with the fire requisite for his future labours. Pursuing the instinct of his nature, he wrought and smelted a portion of his native metal; and, gradually improving his tools, he was able in a few months to begin the construction of another being, framed on the model of himself. This was an arduous undertaking; for, to say nothing of the various joints and members, the mechanism of the heart and lungs consisted of fine springs, chains, and wheels, much like those inside of a watch, — minute net-work, hammers, pivots, bells, and balances. Yet, at the close of a year from his own birth, the second iron man was finished, case-hardened, and polished like glass. Again the storm collected on the mountain-pinnacles; rain fell fast, and hissed in the lake; and lightning filled the air, and streamed and flew over the ground. The vivid flame gathered round the inanimate shape, the workmanship of Chalybs; and, when the tempest cleared away, it rose and moved and spoke, the living type of its parent.

Chalybs, and the adult infant, Ferragus, now worked together; and there was double the smelting, hammering, and filing, that went on before in the valley. The elder of the iron artisans was improved in skill and boldness; and at the end of a twelvemonth four new Siderians were prepared for the animating influence of the electric fire.

From this time the iron population increased in geometrical progression. They were all nearly alike, but with some differences, owing to slight varieties in the quality of the material, and to the fancy of the artisans. In a fit of laziness, hoping to save the labour of the smithy, some of the younger members of the tribe made moulds, and, in different pieces, cast the shapes that they designed to prepare for the stormy anniversary of their race. But some of these figures fell to bits and perished, when the lightning reached them; and the others became such awkward, stupid, inactive beings, that their framers pushed them into the molten lake, where they were fused down to their original condition.

For a considerable period these acts of infanticide were

the only important error that any Siderian was guilty of. They were as happy as they were virtuous; and the only subject that gave them uneasiness, was the difficulty of keeping themselves bright and free from rust. The air indeed of their country was remarkably pure and dry; but no iron would retain a perfect polish, except the tower, which was unaffected by dimness or decay. By the use of the file and of emery however, they contrived for the most part to preserve themselves in their first brilliancy; and before many years they discovered, in the course of their mining, a quantity of rot-stone, which ever after rendered them the greatest assistance.

They grew proud of their continued splendour, and augmenting numbers; and the old simplicity of the Siderians was evidently corrupted. They raised magnificent palaces of shining metal, and even employed their skill in forming arms, toys, and ornaments, of a beauty never found in any other fabrics. They began to talk of constructing a ladder, by which they might reach the summits of the mountains, and conquer whatever regions lay beyond. They were also more and more irritated by the restriction which withheld them from entering the tower. But the advice of Chalybs was more strongly than ever opposed to so rash an undertaking.

At last his descendants began to suspect that he was himself guilty of the crime from which he warned them. They watched him, and discovered that, in secret and lonely hours, he approached the tower, took the key from the hook that supported it, and, having unlocked the door, entered the structure, and remained within it for several hours.

They now broke into open mutiny, said that iron and

steel could no longer bear such tyranny and deceit, and insisted on knowing what was concealed within the turret.

The venerable Chalybs addressed them as follows: "I fear, my children, the hour so long foretold is now come, and that, through my folly and weakness, the race of Siderians is doomed to perish. It is now long since I began to feel that I was no longer the Chalybs I had been of old. My hair was already turning to an iron-grey. It cost me much more trouble than formerly to keep myself from growing rusty; and rust, the enemy of our line, had even, I believe, invaded my vitals. I was in want of some amusement, some consolation; and I could not withdraw my thoughts from the secret hidden in yonder tower. I hoped that my guilt would not be injurious to you; and I crossed the interdicted threshold. I found within; but why should I describe to you what you yourselves shall see?"

He left the assembly, and soon returned, accompanied by a beautiful daughter of that race of clay, which possessed the world beyond the iron valley. On her breast she held an infant; and in its aspect something of the noble Siderian character was mingled with the weakness and softness of its mother.

"From her," said Chalybs, "who is the delight of my life, I learn that the space beyond our native region is peopled by beings like herself. The passage to those wide territories lies through the tower. But remember, my children, that, if you attempt to make use of it, and to pass beyond these mountains, we shall surely perish from the earth."

The iron men, maddened by admiration of the consort of Chalybs, and unchecked by his counsels, rushed to the open turret; whence, passing down an iron stair, and through a long tunnel, the formidable battalion emerged into the dominions of fleshly humanity. They soon provided themselves with brides, and became the early princes of the world.

From their race, mingling with ours, have arisen those potent champions, who, in various ages, have overrun and amazed the earth. From the bodies of the first invaders was derived the invention of armour. They were the smiths who introduced the practice of shoeing horses with metal. The fountains at which they drank, have ever since been called chalybeate, and have preserved a taste of iron. The weapons that they brought with them from their original abode, being discovered in different ages and remote countries, have won the astonishment of mankind for their unequalled size and temper; and a sword, wielded by one of these massive chiefs, became in after ages the national idol of the Scythians.

But the manufacture of iron men has ceased. Chalybs alone clung to his native habitations; and his bride remained with him. He died many years after the dispersion of his tribe; and his semi-human descendants committed his corpse to the lake of its kindred metal. They too then left the valley; and the heavy trap-door closed behind them over the turret-stair. The image of Siderus is said to have rusted, before their departure, into a mass as shapeless as those in its neighbourhood. But, even when many ages had past, the tradition was remembered by the tribes on the other side of the mountains. When after rain the sun shone brightly on the airy precipices, they fancied that the glitter proceeded from one of the iron men, still lingering among the crags of that rocky barrier.

The Substitute for Apollo

(From Arthur Coningsby, 1833)

The eyelids of Jupiter were closed, not in sleep, but inward contemplation. Suddenly his eagle fanned him with its broad wings, and screamed. He opened his eyes, and looked through the crystal floor of heaven at the worlds which were spread below as on a map. He saw mountains shaking down avalanches, and stormy seas, and plains covered with carnage, and palaces filled with crime. He beheld vast deserts tyrannized over by the lion and the serpent, cities where men were wronging and corrupting one another, and all the complication of good and evil. He saw that all was moving in obedience to general laws; and he was undisturbed. But he perceived the corpse of his servant, the Cyclops, on a mountain, and half shaded by the forest, half illuminated by the glare of the volcano. The breast and forehead of the giant were transfixed by the arrows of ethereal fire. The deed had been done by the hand of Apollo, in revenge for the death of his son, whom Jupiter had slain with Cyclopean thunderbolts.

That evening, while the herdsmen and retainers of Admetus were in arms to protect the flocks and cattle of the chieftain against wild beasts and robbers, and were lighting their watch-fires on the Molossian hills, a youth suddenly appeared among them, clad in a rustic dress, with a boar-spear in his hand, and a small stringed instrument slung over his shoulder beside his bow and quiver.

He said that he had lost his way, and should be glad to

remain with them, provided they would furnish him with subsistence in return for his services in hunting and tending cattle. They readily assented to his proposal; and he sat down beside a fire, with the glare of which the last rays of sunset were mingling.

The stranger was Apollo, exiled from the skies by Jupiter, and compelled to take refuge on earth. Fresh from divine converse, the god of poetry knew how to temper himself to the humblest as well as the most exalted natures. Although his eyes were sometimes turned in momentary glances towards that occidental empire, which was now saddening for its departed lord, his jest and roundelay, his narrative of achievements in love and war, and his tales of ghosts and enchanters were delightful to the ears of the peasants round him, and were received with loud applauses, which rang through all the hills, and startled the wolf crouching in the distant brake. He touched his instrument, and sang of the fair nymphs, of the youthful foresters whom they have chosen to live with them in the woods, and of the dogs baying round the thickets which concealed their master, or lying down to die on the verge of the fountain in which he had vanished. His voice then mounted swiftly and clearly towards the stars, and spread like a silver vapour across the valley; and the pause of silent gladness among his auditors was only interrupted by a faint echo of the last notes from the opposite crags and the bare mountain wall.

The god lived on among the shepherds. In every hunting match he was a bold assistant, in every festival a mirthful companion, on the lonely hill-side a friend, and a sage prophet of the weather. To him was given the honour of laying at the feet of Admetus the head of the wild boar and the wolf, and the choicest portions of the slain stag; and the maidens, as they danced over the knolls, or lingered at the fountain, had their quickest and softest looks for him.

The god comprehended all the thoughts of the mountaineers, excelled in all their arts, sympathized with all their sorrows, and delighted in all their enjoyments. He was filled with the spirit of poetry, which, in whatever region it may be thrown, and in whatsoever forms of being immersed, is itself knowledge and power.

Meanwhile the absence of the deity from the celestial palaces was lamented by their inmates; and Jupiter saw that a gloom had gathered on the faces of the Immortals. He was indignant that the presence of the criminal whom he had banished, should be thus important to his race; and he commanded Hermes to bring from earth some human visitant, who might supply the place of the exile.

The herald thought that, among the chosen companions of Apollo, he should be most likely to find a substitute for him. The rough sandals of a Molossian shepherd were soon treading on that crystal floor, into which jewels of all hues seemed to have been melted; and his rude limbs and weather-beaten features appeared among those translucent forms. At first the peasant remained silent and trembling; but, when he had drunk of the mighty wine, he began to talk of flocks and fields, and to express contempt for Admetus, whom he compared in his thoughts with the radiant beings around him. He awoke stupefied and staring among his brethren on his native hills, and uttered broken ravings against his master, which were repaid by blows and curses.

Hermes next introduced a lawyer, who had just reached

his home triumphant after gaining an important cause. His conversation was full of contemptuous jests and eager contradictions. He wrested the laws of the universe to prove that evil is good, and good evil. Hermes therefore conducted him again to earth, and gave him an ample purse of gold, as a fee. But, when the lawyer attempted to use the coin, he was apprehended for passing money not recognised by the state, and put on his trial. He made a long and brilliant speech, in which he described all that had happened to him, not omitting to report his own conversation; and he so well convinced the judges, that the priests of Jupiter were authorized to appropriate the money which had come from heaven.

The next candidate for the throne of Apollo was a soldier. He entered completely armed, as he had been found on his post. He looked with admiration at the helmet of Pallas, and the shield of Mars, and was dazzled by the resplendent beauty of the goddesses. But that presence and that banquet admitted not of repose; and for exertion there was no object. He sat confused and silent, until the goblet did its office, and he sank into heavy slumber. When he recovered his consciousness, he felt the night-wind on his brow, and was keeping ineffectual ward before the camp.

An orator from the public assembly was then presented; and he, when he had tasted of the wine-cup, arose, laid his hand upon his breast, and, discoursing in smooth rhetoric of himself and the deities, showed by much argument and many illustrations, that his most becoming demeanour towards them would be one of modest humility. But before he reached the peroration, he found himself addressing the assembled people, who were delighted at hearing those epithets applied to them, which the speaker had designed for the gods.

The orator was followed by a philosopher, who earnestly looked and listened, and seemed to meditate in what region of his system he should place his new associates. He gazed at all in turn, and asked some questions, from which it was evident that he deemed each a mere abstraction, or pure expression of a principle. When he had mastered, as he believed, the difficulties connected with these transcendent natures, he considered for some time, and then proceeded to explain the laws of refraction and reflection, by which the wondrous light that surrounded him might be accounted for. He enumerated what he supposed were the chemical ingredients of the nectar, assigned its musical character and name to the voice of each of the deities, and analysed the relation they bore to mortals, and that in which mortals stood to them. He was transferred to a blank nook of the universe, where he might study all orders of existence, himself unconnected with any.

Hermes in despair then set a lovely child upon the throne, whom he had conveyed from a valley where she was gathering flowers. The first drop of the immortal liquor which passed her lips destroyed her life; and the messenger was commanded no longer to punish men by bringing them among the deities.

But suddenly the eagle spread its wings and flew to earth, and perched upon a rock which overhung the sea. To the distant mariner the light that surrounded its beak and talons appeared a watch-fire or a meteor. The rock was beside the mouth of a deep cave, in which a poet was musing, modulating his vast melodies to the sound of winds and sea, and revolving his orbed thoughts.

The poet looked upon the bird, and knew that it belonged to a kingdom whereof he was himself a rightful inhabitant. He laid his garland upon its head; his limbs quivered with a sudden lightness; and side by side they rose into the furthest skies. He placed himself upon the vacant throne as upon his natural seat; and the gods recognised in him the mortal who was worthy of celestial converse. He gazed with delighted but undazzled eyes on the forms of beauty and of power: for the art, which in him was impulse and intuition, made him comprehend and feel wherein was the glory, and what the sanctity of those superhuman beings, to whom he knew himself the destined equal.

Balthazar

(From Arthur Coningsby, 1833)

In one of our great English abbeys, long before the reformation, there was a young novice, whose rapid progress in learning, and skill as a musician, made him an especial favourite with the monks, his instructors. It was predicted by them that he would rise to the highest reputation in the church, and perhaps become a bishop, or even a cardinal. This praise-worthy youth was particularly delighted with the study of knotty and abstruse questions, and he sometimes proposed difficulties to the fathers, which it gave them no little trouble to answer. In these cases. Father Timothy, to whom he chiefly addressed himself, was accustomed to advise that Nicholas should cease to think of the subjects which perplexed him, and read his breviary with redoubled diligence. But the young man was so unfortunate as to find great difficulty in turning away his mind from points which he did not understand, and Father Timothy could only lament that his pupil was harassed by the wiles of the devil.

It happened that on a high festival of the church, Father Timothy preached a sermon to which the mind of his pupil gave its most earnest attention. But his eyes unhappily wandered to one of the windows in which were painted a rose of the most brilliant red, surrounded by yellow points, as if of a star, these symbols being known as the pentalpha, and the rose of the hermetic philosophers, and beneath these a man's head, which still bore traces of youth and beauty.

The novice could not help meditating during the pauses of the discourse on these remarkable emblems. But he could form no conception of their meaning. He thought of them in the cloisters, and in his bed, but still he was completely at a loss. He next applied to his instructor, but the only answer he could gain was a severe rebuke for attempting to be wise above that which is written. At last he spoke to an old lay-brother, who informed him of a tradition which he had heard in his youth with regard to what was called Abbot Ingulph's window. It was said that the stained glass was made by the hands of the abbot whose name it bore. He had been much addicted to the occult sciences, and people seldom spoke of him but in a whisper, and with a look of fear. When he was dying, he desired that at his burial the head of his coffin might be laid exactly under the spot to which the bright image of the rose in the window should be thrown by the moonlight at twelve o'clock on the night of the full moon next ensuing.

The temporary successor of the deceased abbot was a man of the most rigid piety, and, instead of complying with this request, he directed that the body should be laid in the ante-chapel beside that of the last buried superior. The coffin was disposed accordingly. But the morning after the funeral, it was found on the spot which had been so singularly pointed out, and the grave designed for it had been filled up. It was again committed to the earth, and again it was found upon the floor of the chapel in the same place as after the first attempt. The baffled father was resolved to persevere; but at the third burial, at the moment when the coffin was lowered into the dust, he took the precaution of touching it with the consecrated wafer. Every one observed the ceremony, trembling and in silence, and the assemblage heard a groan, which sounded as if it had been called forth from the corpse by the immediate agency of the blessed host. The coffin was hastily drawn up again, and the lid forced open, when it was found to contain nothing but a handful of ashes, and a small gold plate, marked with the device of a rose and star. The lay-brother also informed Nicholas that various manuscripts of Abbot Ingulph were said still to exist in the library.

This account wrought, says the legend, in the brain of Nicholas, like the potent ingredients of an adept's crucible. He spent day after day in the library, and found at last an ancient chest, the corners of which were secured by brazen clasps, exhibiting respectively the figures of the toad, the crow, the dragon, and the panther. It was not locked, but sealed, and the wax bore the impression of a man standing on a snake. The young man did not hesitate to break it open, and examined the writings which it contained. They were all works of Abbot Ingulph, except one small thin volume, in which the characters seemed to have been originally so strange, and were now so defaced by time, that Nicholas could not decypher a single syllable. Acting, however, on a hint given in a commentary of the abbot's, he secured this mysterious book, and watched it daily with a longing and almost sickening anxiety, till the night of the full moon. He then stole the keys of the church, and at midnight held the open volume in the crimson radiance which streamed through the rose. The writing instantly became legible; and Nicholas learned the secret for which he had hungered.

For the rest of that night he had in his cell, as the

companion of his studies, a youth, dark-eyed, pale, slow of speech, but master of all the sciences of the world, and of all the languages ever spoken by the bricklayers of Babel, as well as of that rarer tongue, the origin of them all, which is now understood only by the chiefs of the Freemasons.

The next morning Nicholas presented his new friend to the fathers, and proposed that he too should become an acolyte. Balthazar, for so he chose to be called, was examined by Father Timothy as to his proficiency in learning, and in the course of his answers, quoted as one of Christ's replies to the Devil during his temptation, a verse not recorded by St. Luke. The monk referred to the passage, and Balthazar quietly remarked that the Evangelist's account of that occurrence is very inaccurate. This heretical reply decided the holy father to refuse the candidate admittance.

He immediately quitted the monastery. That evening at vespers, Nicholas did not present himself; he could not be found in his cell, nor in the neighbourhood of the abbey. About a year after his disappearance two young Englishmen attracted great attention as disputants in the schools at Paris; and journeyed thence to the monastery of St. Rufus in Provence, where they were soon admitted to full orders. For some years they travelled from country to country, and became celebrated for their learning and talents. They were both of them powerful in discourse on all subjects, but it was observed that Nicholas disliked to debate questions in demonology, which his companion particularly delighted and excelled in, and of which he spoke in a tone of the utmost familiarity.

Their last place of residence was Rome, and here

Nicholas speedily rose to high dignities, while his friend refused to accept any other office than that of his secretary. In this humble situation Balthazar was still sufficiently conspicuous; a thousand dark intrigues for the most extravagant objects were seen to succeed, nobody could tell how, but it was said they had been directed by Balthazar. Innumerable scandals among the enemies of the Cardinal of Alba, for such was now the rank of Nicholas, were detected, while he himself maintained a splendid reputation; and still men whispered and pointed at Balthazar, whenever, that is, they were secure of not being observed by him.

At length the supreme See was vacant. And now discoveries multiplied every hour, so as to implicate the characters of all the leading cardinals. The mistress of one of them became devout, and confessed her own and her lover's immorality; and she was said to be a penitent of Balthazar's. A heretic was burned; when at the stake he cried aloud that one of the Monsignori had first seduced him from the true faith; and it was reported that Balthazar, on the eve of the execution, had gained admittance to the cell of the criminal. A third dignitary of great influence in the college suddenly deserted his former faction, and deprived them of several votes. He was known to have received fifty thousand crowns; and Balthazar was rumoured to have been seen carrying weighty bags under his gown in the direction of the prelate's palace. And lastly, amid the utmost excitement of the election, the French ambassador died, and left the interests of his party in irretrievable confusion. His physician had purchased drugs at a shop, the owner of which was said to have been in the service of Balthazar.

The Cardinal of Alba became pope under the name of Adrian IV. His secretary was his chief counsellor. The defeat and death of Arnold of Brescia were brought about by his wisdom; and it was he who drew up the bull which authorised Henry II to conquer Ireland. But those who were nearest to the pontiff perceived that he feared Balthazar as much as trusted him. A window, exhibiting among other emblems the hieroglyphic rose, had been put up in one of the apartments of the pope. In this room he received Frederic King of the Romans, who, though he entered Italy at the head of a large army, had consented, on first meeting the sovereign priest, to hold his stirrup while he mounted on horseback. Important negotiations were carried on in the presence of the pope and the monarch, and on one occasion Adrian seemed inclined to concede a point of considerable weight, which Balthazar had before maintained with the most resolute firmness against the counsellors of the king. Frederic thought he observed the secretary point slightly to the painting in the window. At all events, the pontiff groaned, turned pale, and trembled; and after a few moments declared his determination to yield nothing.

When Adrian was dying, Balthazar desired that he might speak to his master in private. The patient hesitated, and faltered some words which could not be understood. But the secretary entered the chamber, and the universal bishop shuddered under his look, and feebly motioned to the attendants to retire. In half an hour Balthazar reentered the antechamber, and a slight smile might be observed to hover on his lip. He turned, however, gravely to the domestics, physicians, and cardinals, and pointed to the door through which he had just come. They found the pope dead, with an expression of extreme agony on his lifeless features. A cabinet of steel, inlaid with gold, which stood near the bed, and had before been shut, was now open, and a small parchment volume lay under the hand of the deceased pontiff.

The book was seized by the eldest cardinal present, who attempted to discover its contents. But they were completely illegible, save that near the foot of the last page was found inscribed in bold and youthful characters the name of Nicholas, and lower down, and as if traced by trembling fingers, the regal signature of Adrian. The aged prelate secretly committed the volume to the fire, and was horror-stricken by the groans and sobs which accompanied its destruction, and by the likeness of a demoniac face, which seemed to scowl at him through the cloud of sulphury smoke. Balthazar appeared no more; and it was whispered in Rome that the body of the pope was flung into the Tiber, while, to avoid any open scandal, a coffin filled with rubbish was decorated with the blazonry of Ecclesiastical empire, and buried beside Eugenius III in the church of St Peter.

Beatrice

(From Arthur Coningsby, 1833)

Beatrice, the daughter of a farmer in the north of Italy, was of a bold and ardent disposition, lively and affectionate, conscious of beauty, and fond of power. She was still very young, when her father's feudal superior, the lord of the estate on which she lived, was visited by his brother Ugo, a man at that time nearly of middle age, with high fame as a military commander, of a reserved and haughty temper, and those impetuous passions which the habit of authority, and the licence of his profession, tended to foster. He accidentally saw Beatrice, when in her gayest dress she attended the neighbouring church on the occasion of his presenting at its altar three standards which he had captured in battle. He soon found, or contrived, some opportunity of conversing with her, and thenceforth they met frequently and in secret. Ugo was soon amazed at the indications of a pride as resolute and aspiring as his own; but it rendered her in his eyes the more remarkable and interesting. She attached herself devotedly to him, without having fixed on any course of future conduct. And in the perplexity arising from her situation, and from the struggle of feelings which alarmed while they gratified her, she had recourse to the assistance which human blindness and sinfulness are ever ready to derive from superstition. At a small town, a few leagues from her abode, lived a man whom the people called a magician, but who claimed for himself only the superior wisdom obtained by pious studies, and continued self-mortification. She visited him alone and at night-fall, and told him enough of her story and her wishes to enable him to guess at more. She asked him what were the secret thoughts of her lover with regard to her, and what was the obstacle to her union with him. "Pride," answered her adviser, "is the demon of his soul, as it is the dark ruler of your own. Can you suppose that he, the high-born and powerful, the leader of armies, the counsellor of princes, will ever think of you but as a means of transitory and vicious enjoyment? It is true that he loves you. When he is by your side, he seldom fails to consider how well that unhonoured forehead would be graced by a coronet of pearls, and that the blood of thirty generations of nobles could not flow in a fairer bosom. But that a peasant girl should be more to Ugo than a servant or a paramour, an implement or a toy, is as impossible as that the war-horse he rides should permit itself to be mounted and guided by the dwarfish idiot whose blunders and awkwardness furnish him with occasions of idle merriment." The haughtiness and violence of Beatrice now burst out. She threatened, commanded, wept, and at last implored the magician to gratify her wishes, and find means of raising her to that rank in which alone Ugo would ever look for a partner of his life and glory. "Listen," answered the recluse: "I have been wronged by Ugo, and to ensure his destruction I would willingly devote the toil of many years. This design could in no way be so certainly successful as by my compliance with your wishes. The gratification of them will be the inevitable cause of ruin and disgrace to both of you. If, knowing this, you still persist in your request, you will find me ready to grant it." She smiled scornfully at the thought that a union with one who loved him so fondly could be the means of injury to Ugo, and, with kindling eyes and eager tongue, she declared her willingness to incur all danger in pursuit of her object. "Drink this," said the old man, giving her a potion, "and before long your wishes will be accomplished." She returned home, and in the next morning the young, the beautiful girl was found in her chamber an ice-cold corpse. Ugo soon left the neighbourhood, and plunging into the career of politics, went to the court of a sovereign who had often been defended by his arms and guided by his advice. He was here received with delight by an illustrious nobility, and among them found one whom he had never seen before, the Countess Angelica. He met her for the first time at a masked ball, where his manner towards her, and every other woman, was singularly cold and indifferent. But as she spoke he became more and more attentive; and entering into conversation with her, his voice was full of anxiety while he urged her to remove her mask. In the midst of a blaze of lights and surrounded by persons who, with splendid dress and graceful forms, still served but as a foil for her attractions, she complied with his request; and while she uncovered her face, and fixed on him her bright black eyes, his plumed hat fell from his hand, his complexion was altered by a sudden paleness, and he started one or two paces back. She turned away with apparent carelessness, and in a few moments Ugo recovered himself sufficiently to observe her with keen but silent scrutiny. There was the face, the stature, and the shape of Beatrice, and her animated and noble expression. But for the rustic accent, the woollen garb, the coarse shoes, and ornaments of tawdry silver, he now found nothing but the refined perfection of courtly elegance. The long hair was braided with strings of pearl; and lace, and silk, and golden tissue seemed as if they attempted, unsuccessfully, to conceal a neck and arms that could never have been exposed to the glare of an Italian sun. She appeared at the palace of her sovereign with irresistible evidence that she was the long-lost daughter of a ducal house, and had been educated in a convent at Vienna. In her conversation with Ugo, she had alluded casually to the castles, the estates, and vassals of her family; and had touched on the persons and factions of the court with such light, good-humoured mockery, as proved her intimate knowledge of the highest classes in Europe. Ugo soon entered into the train of her wooers, and before many months was the successful one. A year or two passed on, and he gained new additions to his fame and influence, which involved him more deeply in the dark and perilous politics of Italy. He became more restless, more ambitious than ever; and those difficulties and anxieties which, in their last excess, level the strong mind to the weak, led him to consult the sage on the course of his future fortunes. Ugo visited him in secret, and on hearing the few facts which were all that the statesman would confide to him, "How vain," exclaimed the seer, "are these attempts at concealment! I know you, Lord of Marqua; and I could read your mind even when I was the inhabitant of another hemisphere. Nay, not I alone, who derive wisdom from sources not open to ordinary men, can look through your disguises, and count the pulses of that busy breast, beneath the triple mail with which you cover it. One whom you scarcely deigned to regard as of the same kind with yourself, a peasant girl, through my aid, penetrated your meaning, baffled your designs, and made you her husband. Remember Beatrice, and ask the Lady Angelica in what she differs but in name from the village-maiden, your brother's vassal, whom you sought to bring to shame, and who is now mother of the heir to your titles and your territories. Within the folds of that cloak with which you shade your face so closely, lurks the fiend, your Pride. It will surround you with insane delusions, wither your happiness, and lead you a maniac to the tomb. At last, do you begin to recognise the voice of him whom you so deeply injured? I have, then, told you enough; and now we meet no more, until we shall both have traversed the regions of the grave." From that hour Ugo treated his wife with sullen and fierce disdain. Hers was not a temper to endure scorn, and she purchased vengeance by informing the agent of a neighbouring potentate of the most secret and dangerous schemes of Ugo. Her husband entering, with drawn sword and fixed brow, found them together, and slew them side-by-side. Thenceforth his perturbation increased daily, until he sank into a dull insanity, only broken by fits of drivelling and grotesque dotage.

Land and Sea

(From Blackwood's Magazine, 1838)

I

Jane Martin was the only daughter of a yeoman living in the village of Meadham, not far from the southern coast of England. The place was divided from the sea by a low range of hills; and the fields of pasture and of corn were surrounded by extensive woods. These, together with the small collection of cottages, and the village church, presented a prospect of tranquillity and beauty.

Jane was the heiress of a cottage and a few fields, and, without these advantages, had beauty enough to attract more than one rustic lover. But none of them could win her affections. Her mother had died early, but had left on her daughter's mind a tinge of her own imaginative character. Her father was possessed of some books, which he was fond of reading, and delighted to put in her hands. But he saw that there was mixed up in her disposition a strong portion of the irregular and fantastic strain, which the old man used to say she must have had from her mother, who always, he would add, had been a sort of fairy body, rather than of common flesh and blood like himself. Whatever touch of superstition Jane could light on in his books of history or travels, or in the belief and stories of her neighbours, had a powerful charm for her. Dreams, and prophecies, and accounts of ghosts and visions filled her with awe. When she was about fifteen, and was taken by her father to hear the preaching of a wandering Methodist, a man of coarse but fervid eloquence, the descriptions in which he rioted, of the bodily torments of the lost, and the never-ending delights of heaven, were for her an exquisite, unimagined contrast to the calm morality and grave devotion of the parish church. The effect of this evening, — for the sermon was delivered after nightfall in a dimly-lighted barn, — was so overpowering, that she seemed for some days in a restless fever, and at last was seized with illness. She rose however from her bed apparently strong and fresh as before. Her beauty had lost nothing of its attractiveness, and had gained something in expression. But she did not look formed for happiness. The sensitive and excitable movement of her face, and the quick and striking dilation of the pupils in her large light eyes, conveyed the notion of a mind too early disturbed, and too little under the government of any settled principles of action, for the hope of usefulness and peace. But surrounded as this countenance was with pale brown hair, and supported by a figure of healthy, youthful elasticity, the whole picture of the girl had an affecting sweetness.

Her favourite reading was an old collection of voyages and travels, filled with records of gainful and warlike adventurers, their intercourse with foreign cities and savage tribes, crimes, sufferings, wonders, and superstitions. On these she mused at every moment which she could save from the care of her household affairs and of the dairy and garden. She knew nothing of the world, except within a circle of four or five miles around her father's house; and all beyond presented itself to her mind as made up of sparkling seas and spicy islands, gorgeous towns, and beautiful and heroic men, — ships so light and gay as might sail among the clouds, and cargoes of gold and fruits as glittering as those summer clouds themselves. But, though within seven miles of the coast, she had never seen the sea; and the wish to behold that unknown boundless miracle of nature became, when she had grown out of childhood, the strongest feeling of her mind. Her mother, she knew, was the daughter of a seaman, and had spent her unmarried life at Southport, a town and harbour some twenty miles from Meadham, where her father found his future bride. Now the long-buried mother, whose grave was in the church-yard, and met her eyes every Sunday, appeared to her in her dreams as wearing some indistinct sea-shape, as treading lightly on the waves, and beckoning her to come to that new and delightful region. The thought was too precious to be spoken of to her father; and the girl cherished it, till she half persuaded herself that something more than fancy had shaped the image. For months she turned the wish over and over, till it grew into a project. The notion of some unaccountable good to be derived from looking on the sea, — of some magical beauty clothing the great element, — and of some mystery connected with the moment of her success in the enterprise, fastened on her imagination with no less strength than would on many minds the hope of mounting from earth to one of the heavenly bodies. The plan however seemed almost impracticable. Her father was growing old, a little peevish at any opposition to his will, and more and more settled in his daily round of habits. He was impatient at his daughter's absence, except when he visited his fields and gave directions to his one labourer, a business which seldom occupied more than an hour at a time. The old man was kind and sagacious. His slightest peculiarities were dear to her; and no image she had ever seen with her bodily eyes was to her so agreeable as that of the grey-headed and weather-beaten face. But often, while she sat beside him and supplied his little wants, or answered his few and simple observations, her thoughts would wander away to the restless boundless sea, with all its shores and ships; and the little world around her, for which alone she had outwardly lived, and which alone she knew, seemed poor and small, compared with the dazzling and amazing world of which she knew nothing. She naturally avoided to express her feelings, which she was aware were stronger and more unusual than her father, or any of her acquaintance, could understand or would approve. But the books which he found her reading, and the questions she sometimes ventured to ask as to the seaport town which he had visited in his earlier life, in part betrayed her. One day during such a conversation he suddenly exclaimed, "Heaven help thee! the sea seems always running in thy head! I should not wonder if the first idle sailor that comes wandering here catches thy foolish fancy, and carries thee off from all our honest country fellows. But take care, Jane, — they are an unsteady, spendthrift, drunken set. At best their trade keeps them many a long month in every year away from their wives and children. Don't marry a sailor, Jane; don't marry a sailor; or thy old father will break his heart."

This advice was not very likely to change the current of Jane's thoughts. Her longing to look upon the sea grew rather the stronger; but to gratify it was not easy. The summit of the hills which bounded that inland country, was not further off than two hours' walking; but this was through unfrequented paths and lonely sheep-tracks up the downs. The village lay on no line of traffic with the coast; and to undertake an expedition to the shore without some purpose of business would have sounded among her neighbours like setting off on a crusade or a pilgrimage. She shrank from owning her beloved secret even to her father; and nothing therefore remained but to plan a clandestine excursion. This was only possible at night. A ramble of the kind however had nothing very alarming for a country girl. The imaginative apprehensions, which alone presented themselves to the mind of Jane, added to the charm, by enhancing the dignity of her enterprise. Spirits, she thought, must needs be peculiarly her attendants on the most momentous occasion of her whole life, which had now reached the mature age of eighteen.

The moon was shining in the summer sky, when she crept through her chamber-window, and sprang lightly on the ground. Had any one seen her, it must have seemed, from the excitement of her look and manner under the homeliness of her dark dress, that she was bent on a different kind of meeting from that which she really meditated. She traversed the little garden, and went on by well-known paths, which led her away from the village, and under the shade of hedges and coppices. Rapidly and with beating heart she walked through quiet fields of corn, and began to think that she was now escaping all danger of interruption. In an hour she reached the less cultivated and less populous tract, which divided the plain from the upland. Here she heard from behind her the church-clock, which she knew so well, striking midnight. The path was no longer familiar to her; but she knew the direction she had to take; and her task increased in seriousness and interest, the more completely she appeared engaged in it. The downs arose grim and grey before her; and, after exploring for a few minutes, she struck into the path that climbed their sides, and felt that she had entered on a new world. But she began to be a little fatigued, and mounted the hills with less quickness than she crossed the valley. Still she met no human being. The moon was rising above her head, and displayed her road; and she thought that she perceived the fresh sea-breeze blowing down from the heights upon her face. As she drew nearer and nearer to this aerial summit, which she had so often looked at almost with tears, she could hardly believe the reality of her happiness. In spite of her weariness, her heart was borne up with wings. She paused for a moment a few yards below the top of the ascent, and then ran headlong on, — and stopped.

There lay the sea beneath her, one sheet of indistinct grey and moonshine, with the dark land running off on each side. In the obscurity an angelic vision moved along, with the moon glancing on its white face; it must be, — could it be? — a ship! She felt how deep her own emotions were at the aspect of immense and unknown power, though she could not have explained the cause. The excitement of her mind did not fail after its first rise, but varied and prolonged itself during her minuter examination of all that lay before her. The moonbeams shifted slowly, as the luminary journeyed on and stooped towards the horizon. Here and there the stars were faintly reflected in the gauze-veiled mirror. The ship passed on in silent ghostliness, and disappeared; while the weak murmur of the waters on the shore beneath came to her as if whispering a secret which she vainly strained her ear to catch. She stood charmed to the spot, until the first glimpses of the early dawn began to mingle with the gleams of night. And now she drank in, with a mighty insatiable thirst, each moment of the great unfolding vision. The brightening clouds, — the strengthening breeze, — the cold sad sparkling of the sea under the eye of day, — the colouring of the landscape, and the starting into clearness of many vessels, — all these were memorable events to Jane. But the weariness of the body and the exhaustion of the over-excited mind compelled her to rest; and by the increasing light she saw, a few yards beneath her, a small hollow in the hill, marked by an old thorn-tree which shaded a few large stones. On one of them she sat, and watched the scene before her, till, in spite of her efforts, her eyes closed against the light, and her head drooped sideways against the bank.

❚❚

Jane had lost all consciousness, and was recalled from sleep only by a voice, at which she started; and the first object that caught her eyes, was a young man, who stood before her with the broad sunshine streaming like a glory round his face, and with a figure so graceful, and an attitude of surprise so lively, that Jane, in the midst of her fear, could not but think him the most beautiful object she had ever seen. It was a young sailor, who had taken off his hat to enjoy the air, while climbing up the steep cliffs, and whose exclamation on seeing the sleeping girl had disturbed the dreams of her native village and her cottage hearth.

"No offence, I hope, young woman; but I could not help calling out when I found you here, where I expected only the old thorn-tree."

"Oh, no," she answered, "it is my fault, — that is, I believe I have been asleep, and it is very wrong."

"Well, I do not see much harm, unless you had fallen asleep when it was your watch on deck; and you're hardly a sailor yet. But, if I may make so bold, it must be something out of the way that brings you here at this hour of the morning. The sun is not above half an hour up. I have been this way pretty well at all hours; and I never found any one here yet but an old shepherd, and perhaps sometimes of an evening a pair of sweethearts; and you are none of the neighbours; — I know them, young and old, for three miles round."

Then came the explanation of Jane's adventure; and, in telling it slightly as she did, there was to her own feelings a strain of extravagance in it, which she had never perceived till now, when she was compelled to speak of it. The stranger was full of wonder; but he thought, from her look and manner, she must be telling the truth. His determination to find out how this was, gained strength perhaps from her personal charms; for the rounded active figure and the soft face, with her bright eyes, and long pale hair curling from under her bonnet, were not lost on one who in his voyages had seen many a pretty maiden, but never a prettier than Jane Martin. He immediately proposed, as he had no business that could not wait, to take care of her back to her father's. She refused with a deep blush and downcast look, and, wishing him a good morning, had turned to go; but her steps faltered, partly, doubtless, from fatigue. In a moment the young sailor was at her side, and insisted that she was too weak to return without his help. The arrangement was soon made; and at four o'clock in the morning the pair set off on their walk, which, according to Jane's design, ought to have ended about the same hour.

The road however was now down hill. She had succeeded in the greatest aim she had ever conceived; and her companion's arm was of much assistance. Jane discovered, in the first half-hour of their acquaintance, that he was the son of a fisherman's widow, living in a cottage at the foot of the cliff. He had early gone to sea, and now, at the age of twenty-two, had risen to be second mate of a merchantman, in which he had made a voyage to the Mediterranean. On returning to England, he had been on a visit to his mother, and had set out that morning to walk across the country to Southport, where he hoped again to obtain employment, and perhaps in a better situation than his last. After several other questions and replies, "How," she said, "do you pass the hours, when there is nothing to be done in the ship?"

"I read or sing, or think of my friends at home; and I fancy that some day or other there may be some one on shore, younger and prettier than my poor mother, who may remember me when I am away, as I should remember her."

If Jane had been a lady, she would hardly have answered, "Well, when I have nothing to do, I mostly think of the sea, and how men pass their lives upon it, and what sights they have to look at."

"And all this, though you have no friend a sailor, — no brother or cousin, or lad that you used to play with when you were both children?"

She blushed, and said, "No, — no one. My mother's father was a sailor; and I have read of many more in books; but I never saw one to speak to before."

"And have you never thought if you would like to have a friend who had made many a voyage? Would it not be pleasant to be able to fancy that one you knew was on the wide waves, and thinking of you while you would be remembering him? — some one whose return you would look for, and who would bring you new stories every trip, of all he had fallen in with, and perhaps some pretty trifles, and gowns and lace, from foreign parts?"

It was with a low deep longing voice that she answered, "Oh, that would be too much happiness!" Then she hung her head, and hid her face from him, but leaned the more clingingly on his arm. In truth she was almost overpowered by fatigue and want of sleep; and they were now at last within a stone's-throw of her father's door. She turned from the lane they were walking in, and passed over a stile into one of his fields; and when they reached the orchard behind the cottage, she begged William to remain at its little gate, while she went forward, for she did not know in what state she might find her father on account of her absence. He remained leaning on the gate for a few seconds, till startled by a woman's scream, when he hurried in, and, pushing through a passage which contained three or four persons, all in confusion, he found himself in the old man's bedroom. There were several neighbours round the bed, on which he lay apparently insensible; and Jane stood supporting herself by one of the bed-posts, and with her eyes fixed on his face. William went to her side, and saw the closed eyes gradually open, and the father begin to see. The first objects he beheld were his daughter, and the young man standing by her in his sailor's dress. He looked at them long and sadly, and at last muttered, "I was sure it would be so."

Jane now begged that she might be left alone with her father, who was used to her attendance, and specially requested William, as he was a stranger, to stay in the outer room till she could go and speak to him. Reluctantly, and shaking their heads, the neighbours went away. The father was still very feeble; and it was only after long delay, broken by floods of tears from her, that she could communicate the story of her own proceedings, and could learn what he had to tell. On getting up, and not finding her in the house, he had hurried about his premises, and, still missing her, had alarmed the nearest neighbours, and sent in different directions to look for her. But when two or three of the messengers returned without any tidings, he had fainted away; and a crowd had gathered round him, as he lay on his bed, the moment before Jane arrived. In an hour he felt sufficiently strong to rise; and he and his daughter went to rejoin the sailor, and offered him breakfast, of which they partook with him. But his fresh and lively look was very different from the stern sadness of the father, and from Jane's deep and confused dejection. He was not discouraged however from speaking, nor she from listening. Even the old man relaxed into civility before he took leave.

It was not many days till he came again; and Jane soon learned that he had put off his journey to Southport. Thenceforth they met frequently; and in the summer evenings he was seen walking about the quiet country lanes with Jane leaning on his arm. It was no surprise therefore to the village, when the banns were read in the church for the marriage of Jane Martin and William Laurence. With slow gestures and thoughtful eyes her father gave her to her husband. They returned to live with him; and in the first glad flush of their love the old man died. His death was a shock to Jane, but not a lasting grief. She loved William too fully and entirely, to feel any gap in her life while she possessed him; and though she would have been ready to toil for her father's comfort, had he lived, his death was far from overpowering her. Nay, — though it is a severe truth, — she felt relieved from his silent forebodings, and seemed to belong more entirely to William, now that all other claims on her had ceased.

Not long after this, William's mother was taken ill; and he was sent for to see her. She died before his return; and both were now deprived of all they had much loved beyond each other. In a few weeks it became necessary for William to go again to his former home, in order to sell the furniture and let the cottage; and Jane proposed to accompany him. She rejoiced in the thought of again seeing the place where they had first met, and of knowing more familiarly that ocean which she had obtained so insufficient a glimpse of. They went thither, and took up their abode in the sea-side cottage. All about it spoke of maritime occupation. The house was partly constructed of wreck. The paling round the puny garden was of the broken and pitchy boarding of boats; and the shingle lay driven in barren heaps against it. Within a stone's-throw two or three fishing-boats were drawn up on the beach; and the children of the fishers' families played along the shore. In the cottage there was great want of many of the inland comforts Jane had been used to; but there were a few articles of trans-marine curiosity, brought home by William, such as uncut coral and pink-hearted shells.

Through the greater part of the day the husband and wife were busy in their household affairs, examining and arranging their new possessions. But in the evening they felt more at liberty, and they strolled together along the shore. Jane knew not what it was that attracted her; but she had an obscure notion of a wonderful and friendly power in the sea, as if its movements had been the beatings of a mighty paternal breast, on which she could lay her head. She walked along the outermost line of foam; and every wave that broke delighted her, while at intervals she turned and stood, and looked over the waters with vague but deep emotion. A child who has been gazing at a lovely star, till he almost fancies it his own, would not be more gratified by seeing it suddenly drop from the skies into his lap.

"Jane," said William, "you seem as much pleased as a child with a new toy; yet the sea is not to be joked with. Though there is only a little ripple on it now, I have seen a swell that frightened the best seaman on board; and many a hundred, — ay, many a thousand ships, with all their crews, have gone to the bottom, smooth as you may think it atop. I must tell you some stories of shipwrecks, that you may not fancy it all plain sailing, and may be willing to go back home, away from the surf."

"You need not," said Jane; "I heard plenty such stories from my mother, and I have not forgotten one of them. Besides the woman with the green hair, who appeared to my grandfather, is dreadful enough."

"The woman with the green hair!" said William,

suddenly. "Who saw that? who told you of it?"

"My grandfather saw it twice; and my mother told me of it. He used to make voyages to Holland and Germany, I think; for I remember my mother showing me the places in our old map. Once he had not long left the port, somewhere abroad, when the fog began to thicken round him, and the wind at the same time to rise. The sailors wanted him to turn back; but he would not; for he was a very bold and obstinate man. The weather grew worse and worse; and at last, when he had just refused the advice of all on board to go back into harbour, he saw a figure rise out of the water on the side nearest the wind, and float in the air against the fog, close to the mast. She put out her hands, as if to push him and his ship back; and he noticed her so well, that he could describe her as he could any of his friends. She was young and handsome, in a long grey dress, with pale green hair hanging down over her neck. My grandfather would not heed; and that night his ship was dashed upon the shore, and he lost everything he had. All his crew were drowned; and he was thrown upon the beach himself, almost a corpse."

"Well," said William, "was that all? did he ever see her again?"

"Yes. For some years after, he made successful voyages; and he spoke to his family of the sight he had seen, as of something strange and remarkable, but not as if it had been of any real importance. My mother had heard him describe the figure so often, that she said she felt as if she had seen it herself. After she had been married some months, she went with her husband to pay her father a visit, before he should sail on what he intended should be his last voyage. He had laid out most of his property in a cargo for the vessel, and expected to make a great deal of money by it. The evening before he was to sail, he was returning from the harbour to the house he lived in, a mile or two out of Southport. The way lay along the sea-side; and it was a beautiful summer evening, with a slight sunny mist spread over the water. After he had got clear of the town, he turned round to look at the masts of his ship, which were plain enough to be seen; and he noticed an odd movement, with some faint lines in the sunshine, above the water. It grew clearer and clearer, till he saw that it was the woman with the green hair. He could have thought it not an hour since he last saw her; so exactly was she the same, except that now a weak yellow brightness from the sun fell over her grey dress and pale green hair. She waved her hand and looked at him, so that he understood well enough that she warned him not to go back to the ship. At first, he owned, he was dreadfully frightened; but, as she did not cease her warnings, he turned his head from her, and proceeded on his way. He did not dare look back again, till he had struck into a path that led down a hollow, so that the sea was hidden from him. There was then no appearance of the figure. He came home much changed in his manner; and his face and voice were very sad, when he told his wife and daughter what had happened to him. But he could not afford to give up his voyage; and besides he would not have borne to be laughed at by his friends, as he must have been had he stayed on shore for such a reason."

"And what came of it?"

"My mother never saw him after the next morning, when he went to sea. He was washed overboard and drowned before the eyes of his crew. I was born three or four months after; and my mother was so affected by her loss, and by the story of the green-haired woman, that she thought the impression made on her had given me the same kind of features and look, as those of the appearance described by my grandfather. My hair indeed has never that I know of been green."

William was long silent: at last he said, "Jane, I must tell you what I am thinking of. I heard this story told by an old sailor of Southport, who said he had sailed in the ship, the master of which was lost as you have just related, though I had no notion that he was your grandfather. But I have seen the green-haired woman twice myself. I was in the Mediterranean, and was the mate keeping watch on deck. The night was cloudy; but every now and then we had a good glimpse of moonshine. The moon however was hidden, when I happened to be looking towards the larboard bow, and saw, right abreast of the foremast, hanging against the clouds, the sort of figure you spoke of, with her green hair falling about her. Her body and dress seemed much the colour of the clouds behind, so that I could not make out her shape; but just then a flash of moonshine came, and I saw her as plain as I see you. She seemed, as you said, to be signing to us to change our course. I called one of the seamen to try if he could notice anything in the direction in which I saw her; but at the moment of his turning his head she disappeared. I tried to think no more of it; and an hour after a Greek pirate came up and boarded us with a dozen men; we had to fight for it hand to hand, and lost three lives before we got rid of the scoundrels; and I had a wound in my shoulder that I feel even yet. Now it is strange that the course the figure signed to us to steer, would, as we found the next day, have taken us clear away from the pirate, into the midst of the British squadron of men-of-war. But there is something more curious than this. You say your mother thought you had taken after the build of the figure, from her hearing it spoken of by her father; now, when I saw you the first time that morning up yonder at the lover's seat, the first thing that struck me was, — Well that girl is the likest I ever saw to the green-haired woman. Your hair even had a little greenish look, though that perhaps was from the shade of the old thorn-tree above you. I have never since been able to get it out of my head, that you and she are somehow sisters, though I never saw two sisters so much alike."

Jane laughed, not very heartily, and owned it was strange that he, as well as her mother, should have noticed the likeness. "But you spoke," she said, "of seeing this figure twice. How did it happen the second time?"

"Oh! that was much less remarkable. My old captain made my fortune by promoting me to be a mate, and getting me some education. Soon afterwards he gave up the ship; and, as he was walking home from the town, I went half-a-mile or so with him to bid him good by. I was thanking him for his kindness, when he said he wanted no thanks; but he would be glad if I would promise him one thing, and this was, that, if ever by any chance he went to sea again, I would sail with him. I was looking up in his face, and was saying, Yes, when I saw over his shoulder, above a clump of trees on the top of the down where it looks along the sea, the same figure of the green-haired woman. It was bright sunshine, and I saw her quite plainly.

She was frowning and making signs to me, as if to prevent
me from promising; but I was not to be stopped so easily;
and I gave the old man my word, I would go with him
immediately on his letting me know, unless I should have
taken a berth in another ship beforehand.”

“And would you go now, that you are married?”

“To be sure I would, — I must. Why, what harm should
happen to you when I am away? And we should be all the
better pleased with each other on my return after a four or
five months’ voyage. But I don’t think there is much chance
of it; for the old man has made his fortune, and is not likely
to spend it.”

▌▌▌

The husband and wife returned in a few days from the sea-
coast to their inland farm; and time passed on quietly with
them until their son was born. Young Richard, — for so he
was named, after his maternal grandfather, — was a new
happiness to both the parents. William too had grown
tolerably familiar with rural occupations, and was pleased
with the cultivation of his land. It was now again
midsummer; and the village, with its fields and trees, looked
as beautiful as when Jane set out on her first expedition to
the sea. But how different were her feelings now! It seemed
to her as if in some mysterious way she had, in William,
married the sea itself; and her restless fancies were all
quieted. But this calm was not to last. It was a bright July
evening; and William had come in from the fields, and was

sitting down to his meal with his wife, who was preparing the table, while he danced the child upon his knee, when the postman came to the door with a letter, which, from the rarity of the occurrence, startled them as if it had been a gunshot fired into the room. The father turned pale when he saw the handwriting, and laid the child on the floor. It was a letter from his old captain, saying that he had lost his fortune by an unsuccessful speculation, and was now about to embark on a voyage to Brazil, in which he claimed William's promised help as chief mate of the ship. He saw at once that he must go. Jane spent the evening and most of the night in weeping, while he endeavoured to explain his wishes as to her mode of life in his absence, and the measures she should take for the management of the farm, which, with her active rural habits, did not promise to be a very difficult business. The next morning at daybreak he started from Meadham on his way to Southport; and Jane and her child were left to cheer each other as they might.

The autumn and winter passed on; and with the spring she had the hope of seeing her husband again. But not so was it to be. The spring brightened into summer; but William came not with the leaves and crops. The summer advanced to maturity; but the husband of Jane did not come to reap his harvest. She could no longer endure the sight of Meadham; and, as the sea-side cottage was now again untenanted, she resolved to remove thither, as if, in being nearer the sea, she should be nearer to William. She intrusted her farm to a labourer on whom she could rely, and went with her child to live upon the strange and inhospitable shore. For some weeks she would spend hours in looking over the sea, and watching every vessel; but she grew weary of this habit, and devoted herself to her son. He was growing into a vigorous and lively child; and his likeness to his father perpetually reminded her of the husband she had lost. Her talk with the boy related almost entirely to the life and exploits of seamen; and she seemed to devote him from his infancy to the task of one day following and recovering his parent. Nothing gave her so much pleasure as to see him mingle with the fishermen and their children, and so partly prepare himself for his future life. Once indeed she returned to Meadham for a few days, in order to arrange the affairs of the farm, and took Richard with her. But the delight with which he beheld the inland cultivation, the large trees, the green and yellow fields, and the comparative comfort and spaciousness of the farm-house, so alarmed his mother, that she never let him return there for more than a few hours. Gradually he came to consider the sea as his inevitable destination, and to share in her superstition that, if he but sailed on a distant voyage, he could not fail to find his father. He was about eight years old, when he begged to be allowed to accompany one of the fishermen in his voyage to Southport (where was the market for his fish), and back to the fishing village, — an expedition which in all probability would only last a day. He departed in all the joyousness of childhood; and his mother, who had clothed him in a new dress, like that of a full-grown seaman, and not like that of a fisherman, saw the boat set sail with her son on board, as happily as if he had been going to his wedding. But, while her eyes were still fixed on it, and before it had gained twenty yards from the beach, she discovered, sitting beside the mast, and as it were pushing the child towards the land, the grey figure of a woman with long green hair. She could not be mistaken; it was distinctly visible against the dark red sail; Jane sank back on the shingle, pointing towards it with her outstretched hand. After a long delay she found strength to regain her home, and spent the whole day at the window which overlooked the sea, with her eyes fixed on the point of the headland, round which the fishing-boat would first come in sight. It was a clear and glowing evening close upon sunset, when the dark sail crept into view, and looked a spot of blood in the bright and glassy expanse lighted up by the sun, now setting behind the down from which Jane had first beheld the sea. She now watched the boat that bore her only child: she hardly observed any of the other sails that glided over the waters, most of them at a greater distance than the one she eyed so fixedly. Among these was a square rigged vessel coming from the north into the bay, with coals for the neighbouring population, and pressing on, anxious to save the tide for unloading, so as to leave the unprotected beach on the following morning. Jane knew nothing of this; but, as she continued to observe the boat while it drew on, and the ship advanced in a converging line, and both were hardly now more than a mile away from her, by some mismanagement on both sides the boat was run down. It upset on the instant; and Jane could distinguish one of the two men who were in it clinging to a rope flung from the ship. What became of the other lives she could not see. But for her the event was enough. Connected with her husband's history, and the appearance in the morning, the accident spoke plainly to her mind. After the first horror, she sat motionless with stiffened eyes, till the ship took the ground, when perhaps with some miserable revival of hope, she ran out of the house towards it. The first person she met was the rescued fisherman, who shook his head and dropped his hand before she reached him: she sat down on the beach, stooped her forehead on her knees, and asked him no questions. Before an hour some of the neighbouring women had gathered round her. At last one of them ventured to address her, and, taking courage from her silence, lifted her up in her arms: she made no resistance, but walked quickly to her home. Only on their attempting to lay her on her bed she turned fiercely away, and sat down at the window from which she had witnessed the destruction of the boat.

The women found they could make no change in her determination; for she only answered them by requests that they would leave her to herself. They at last complied; and she remained alone at her open lattice in the deepening twilight. Through it was to be seen the line of coast to the right, with the black ship lying at a quarter of a mile from her, beset with men and wagons engaged in unloading the coals. The shore beyond stretched away in a dark line terminated by the headland, round which she had seen the boat disappear in the morning, and again return scarcely two hours ago. She fixed her eyes upon the water between this promontory and her, and saw them far in the night gradually brighten beneath the moon. It was after midnight when, in this trembling radiance, she discerned a hazy speck hovering above the waves; and, as she gazed more earnestly, it became the woman with the preter-human hair, who was again distinctly marked, and looking mournfully at her. A dark mass seemed rolling before her in the water; and as she and it drew close to the shore, the expression of the sea-woman's face became so piteous, that Jane got up and went to the edge of the water, where, driven at that instant on the shingle, lay the body of her son. She lifted it from the waves, and sat down on the beach with the cold and heavy corpse upon her knees. It was dressed in the new blue clothes which she had made for him with so much pleasure after the model of those worn by his father. The water from them covered her with moisture, over which at last the warm tears fell down, while she felt the dead unresisting limbs, and looked on the pale face and staring eyes. The dark brown hair still hung about the forehead, dripping with the brine, and showing none of the curls which she had so often handled. All else seemed changed; but by long gazing she could still recognise, in the moonshine, the fair boyish features, and lips that never more would smile on her. She could not bear the horny stare of the eyes; and she gently closed the lids before she lifted the body, and walked with it to her home. When there, she called for no help of her neighbours, but laid it on the little grass-plot, while she went and struck a light. She again lifted the burthen, and laid it on her own bed, in which her boy had always slept. She took off the clothes, washed away the sand and salt, stretched him, as if in sleep, where he had been used to lie, and then threw herself beside the senseless clay, and pressed it to her bosom. Passionate grief and floods of tears followed; and then again she lay exhausted and helpless, till her returning strength broke out anew in bursts of misery. At last she was motionless as the corpse itself, and almost equally lifeless. While she was in this state, with her moveless arms hanging round the body, a stranger, in the first grey of the dawn, entered the house, the door of which was unfastened, and saw, by the sickly expiring light, the spectacle of the mother and her dead child. At first he started and shuddered, but soon began to gaze steadily on the pair, till, gathering conviction, he exclaimed, "Jane, Jane, can this be you?"

She raised herself slowly and silently in the bed from beside her child, and looked at the speaker. A minute passed before she cried aloud, "William, I have killed our boy." It was indeed William, returned a broken and haggard man. They spent the following hours in such melancholy talk as became their condition. Jane learned that her husband's vessel had been wrecked on the coast of South America, that he and one or two others had escaped, but had been long detained in the interior, partly by the whites, partly among the Indians, had made several unsuccessful attempts to reach Europe, and only now, after eight years' absence, had arrived in England in a vessel from Monte Video. He had landed at Southport, and hastened to the fishing village, which was hardly out of his road to Meadham, and where he expected to hear some intelligence of his wife and child.

The corpse was borne in its coffin on the shoulders of the fishermen along the path to Meadham; for the cart-road went many miles round. William and Jane walked together behind the bearers up the down, and past the lover's seat where they had first met, and along the whole track on which that summer morning she had been supported by his arm while returning to her father's house. His hair was now grey, but hers was white as snow.